What Bae Won't Do:

The Finale

What Bae Won't Do:

The Finale

Genesis Woods

www.urbanbooks.net

Urban Books, LLC
300 Farmingdale Road, NY-Route 109
Farmingdale, NY 11735

What Bae Won't Do: The Finale
Copyright © 2021 Genesis Woods

ISBN 13: 978-1-64556-204-7
ISBN 10: 1-64556-204-2

First Trade Paperback Printing June 2021
Printed in the United States of America

10 9 8 7 6 5 4 3 2 1

This is a work of fiction. Any references or similarities to actual events, real people, living or dead, or to real locales are intended to give the novel a sense of reality. Any similarity in other names, characters, places, and incidents is entirely coincidental.

Distributed by Kensington Publishing Corp.
Submit Orders to:
Customer Service
400 Hahn Road
Westminster, MD 21157-4627
Phone: 1-800-733-3000
Fax: 1-800-659-2436

What Bae Won't Do:

The Finale

Genesis Woods

Acknowledgments

First and foremost, I want to thank everybody who has been rocking with me since my first release. . . . It's been ten months, and this is book number five. To some, this may not be a big accomplishment, but to me, this means a lot. Being a jack-of-all-trades, I tend to dabble in a lot of different things. Some I keep up with; others I tuck away and forget all about. The fact that I finally chose something from my talent pool and stuck with it is saying a lot about me and the woman I am becoming. Writing isn't "my life" by far, but it is a portion of it that I hope my cubs will one day see and be able to tell their friends about. Anyhoo . . . I know *Bae3* has been a long time coming, but you guys just don't know how hard it is to write a book. I definitely take my hat off to those authors who can spit out a book in a week or two. You definitely deserve kudos for that!

There are a few people I want to give a shout-out to. Some I speak with every day, some I speak to sometimes, and others I just communicate with on FB. You guys don't know how inspirational you are to me. . . . And I appreciate everything! **Tia** (my cousin, my BFF: You die, I die . . . just like that), **Nickey** (my BFF, my Ride or Die for life), **Diamon** (one of my biggest fans: I love your life), **Jessica Wren** (Baby Mama #1: We rocking to the wheels fall off), **Candace Mumford** (IDK where my mental would be without you), **Blake Karrington** (the best boss ever), **Claudia Smith** (BBE fo' life!), **JM**

Acknowledgements

Hart (my Gayle all day, every day), **Geraldine Grady** (Your opinion is always the deciding vote), **Brittney Marx** (my cousin: Your support gives me life).

And I wish to express my gratitude to my readers who stay on my head about writing (y'all know who y'all are). We stay going back and forth on my timeline or in my in-box, some a little more than others (I'm clearing my throat). Tarina Wright (LOL) . . .

To all my friends, family, associates, and enemies who've bought one of my paperbacks and/or downloaded my shit on Amazon, thank you. I love all of y'all!

~Genesis

JaNair

I looked out into the crowd and scanned the faces of the many people who were in attendance. Some I knew, some I'd seen before, and some I wouldn't remember two days from now.

Once again, Jerome had outdone himself with this whole birthday celebration. First, it was the mountain of gifts, and now it was the Las Vegas–style party, which I had said I wanted a while ago.

I turned around and looked at everyone sitting in my VIP section. Despite two other parties going on in this section, we still had enough room to fit fifty more people here.

I looked at Lil Ray and LaLa in the corner, having a heated conversation about all the greasy food she'd been scarfing down since we got here. I laughed at how protective he was toward her and how concerned he was about the types of food she was feeding their baby. Toby and Niecey were on the dance floor, and surprisingly, he was grooving and swaying his hips perfectly to the beat. Who would've thought a white boy could be so smooth? I could tell by the way he looked at her the whole time that they were dancing that he had some type of feelings for her. Niecey's face seemed to be glowing as well. She looked happy. Way happier than I had ever seen her whenever Big Will was around.

My attention turned to Jerome, who was talking to Gerald and his date. At first, I had thought the group dynamics were going to be kind of awkward, being that Gerald and LaLa had hung out before and they were both here with new people, but like Jerome had explained, they weren't meant to be and both of them understood that.

"Hey, Jay. I just wanted to come up here and wish you a happy birthday. This is my friend Genelle. Genelle, this is the birthday girl, JaNair," Ryan said, introducing me to the Ciara look-alike standing next to him.

"Thank you, Ryan. And it's nice to meet you, Genelle."

She shook my hand but didn't say anything. The vibe that I was getting from her felt kind of weird, like she wanted to say something to me, but Ryan had told her not to.

"Um, I hope you don't feel uncomfortable being here," I told her. "Ryan and I haven't dated for a while, and we're simply just friends. His cousin and I are best friends, and since we still see each other sometimes because of her, I invited him to my party."

She shook her head. "No, it's nothing to do with that. I know you are in a relationship with that fine-ass brother right there." She pointed at Jerome, who happened to look up at that moment and smile. "Whew, that man is gorgeous." Ryan cut his eyes at her and started to pull her away, but not before she offered a few parting words. "If I were you, girl, I'd watch my man around all these trifling females. Even family."

I scrunched my perfectly arched eyebrows as I watched her and Ryan walk out of the VIP, arguing. That shit was hella weird, but I got over it quickly.

I went and grabbed my purse and pulled my phone out. Semaj's ass still hadn't texted me back. Since we got here, I'd texted him again, thanking him once more for the gift that he had sent me. I had been overexcited when I opened it up while I was in the bathroom and had seen what it was.

"Happy birthday, cousin," broke me from my thoughts. As much as I didn't care too much for Mya right now, I had extended an invite and was now glad to see that she'd come to the party and was doing okay.

"Thank you, Mya. You look nice tonight." I wasn't lying; she did. The two-piece red crop top and pencil skirt looked good on her. She had on some black pumps, and her hair was in a slick ponytail at the back of her head.

"Thank you, thank you. You look good yourself. Then again, you should since you're the birthday girl, right?"

I nodded my head, not sure if I should take that as a compliment or not.

"What are you drinking?" she asked. "Your next drink is on me."

"Oh no, you're good. Jerome paid for bottle service for the whole night, so I don't need anything else to drink. But check you out, offering to buy me a drink," I said, joking around.

"Is that all you think I can buy you? Because if it is, you're sadly mistaken. I can buy you a bottle, just like Jerome," she said with a smirk on her face.

I didn't know what that was all about, and I never got the chance to ask, because as soon as I opened my mouth, four waitresses walked into the VIP holding a big-ass cake with what looked like a hundred sparklers on it.

"Happy birthday to you. Happy birthday to you. Happy birthday, dear JaNair (BFF, Bae, Baby Mama). Happy birthday to you," everyone sang.

I looked at Toby's crazy ass and shook my fist at him. I didn't know when or why he had started calling me his baby mama. But if Jerome didn't get mad about it, neither would I.

I had just blown out all the sparklers on my cake when Jerome took my hand and got down on one knee. My throat became dry as hell, and my heartbeat started to speed up. I looked at the small circle of people that had seemed to form unnoticed around us.

LaLa, Niecey, Toby, and even Tangie, who had just gotten here, had smiles on their faces. The only person who wasn't wearing one was Mya. She didn't even try to disguise the smug look on her face when we locked eyes.

At that precise moment, events from the past few months began to flash through my mind. The way Mya's ass would twist her face whenever Jerome and I were together stood out. It was either that or she'd say something slick, which usually included Semaj's name somewhere in the mix.

I broke our gaze, but then I looked at her again, and it was obvious that she had some things she wanted to get off her chest. So me being the caring cousin that I was, I just had to find out. Yeah, I was about to ask her in the middle of Jerome's proposal, and low key, I probably could've waited until he was finished. But at this point, I really didn't give a fuck.

"JaNair Simone Livingston, will—" was all Jerome got to say before I cut him off.

"Hey, Mya! What the fuck is your problem?"

All eyes turned to her.

"What do you mean, JaNair? I'm standing here watching your man try to propose to you, like everyone else." She looked around at the crowd, then back at me. When her eyes traveled over to Jerome, he looked at her with a scowl on his face, then quickly turned his head. I took note of that little interaction, then turned my attention back to her.

Something was definitely up with this bitch, and I was about to find out.

I walked up to her with my hand on my hip and invaded her personal space. "I wanna know, what the fuck is your problem? I'm looking around at everybody's face, and I see nothing but smiles. However, when I look at yours, all I see is animosity. Are you angry about something, Mya?"

"She's jealous!" someone yelled while coughing at the same time.

I ice grilled the idiot for a moment, then waited for Mya to answer my question.

She looked at a belly-rubbing LaLa, who was discreetly shaking her head no. She looked at Jerome again, and he avoided making eye contact with her.

"So?" I asked, starting to get the feeling that something was about to pop off.

She smirked. "Yeah, Jay, I have a problem. But it doesn't have anything to do with being jealous of you," she said smugly as she started to walk around me. "You see, my problem happens to be the same one that you have."

I reared my head back and cocked it to the side. "And what problem would that be?"

"Jerome fucking your so-called best friend and possibly getting her pregnant."

The shit she had just said to me didn't really register with me until I saw Lil Ray take his arm from around LaLa and mean mug the hell out of her. She tried to grab his face and say something, but he turned around and stormed out of the VIP section.

I looked over at Niecey and saw Toby firmly grab her arm, trying to keep her from getting to a laughing Mya.

"Baby, please! Let me ex—" was all Jerome managed to get out before my open palm connected with the side of his face. I hit him so hard that his lip started to bleed. The shocked look that he had on his face told me that he had not only heard that shit, but he had felt it too.

"Bitch! Are you crazy?" he yelled as he stalked toward me. Before he could get any closer, Toby grabbed my arm and pushed me behind him.

"Rome, man, you know I will always have your back, and you're like a brother to me. But trying to attack a woman who only reacted to the shit you caused is not gonna fly while I'm here. Let me take you home so you can cool down, and if JaNair's up for talking to you in the morning, you can do it then. Cool?"

After looking around at all the shocked faces, Jerome nodded his head and then turned his attention back to me. I wanted to say something real slick, but I didn't get the chance to due to LaLa's ear-piercing scream.

"Oh my God! I think my water just broke," she moaned as we all rushed to her side.

"Are you all right, LaLa? Do you need anything?" I asked, kneeling in front of her.

She nodded her head and started to scream again. All that concern I was showing her was just an act; I really didn't give a fuck how she was doing, to be honest. I just needed some way to get close to her without her noticing.

After Mya had dropped that little bomb about Jerome possibly being her baby daddy, she knew to keep some space between us. That was why I hadn't got a chance to slap her right after I'd slapped Jerome.

"Are you sure you're okay, LaLa?" I asked, looking her in the face.

When she nodded her head again and gave a quick smile, I nodded my head in return. Before I stood up to give her some breathing room, I raised my arm up and sent my fist flying into her nose. Blood instantly started to gush out. The oohs of some of the guests that were still in the VIP started to echo throughout the confined space.

I didn't even look back to see the damage that I'd done to her face as I grabbed my clutch and jacket. The only thing that was on my mind was getting the hell out of there. My mental was so gone right now, I was liable to beat that damn baby outta her ass.

After making sure I had everything in my hands that I'd come with, I headed out of the club and to the limo. Not even caring that the driver was obviously on a smoking break, I jumped in the back of the sedan and slammed the door shut.

"Uh . . . where to, ma'am?" he said as he sat in the driver's seat.

"LAX."

He turned around and looked at me. "You don't want to wait for the rest of your—"

"No! LAX please," I said, interrupting him, as I closed the partition.

Once it finally registered with this fool that I didn't give a fuck that we were leaving the rest of my party behind, he put the key in the ignition and revved up the engine.

When the limo started to move, I opened up my clutch and took out my birthday gift from Semaj. A small smile formed on my face as the round-trip ticket to Texas stared back at me.

I'm on my way, J2, and I'm really ready this time, I said to myself. Closing my eyes, I let thoughts of tonight's event and the prospect of seeing Semaj's smiling face lure me to sleep.

LaNiece

"Agggh!" I cried out, as I was in so much pain. Not only was an insane amount of blood gushing out of my nose, thanks to JaNair, but these contractions I was having every ten minutes had me ready to die.

"LaLa, I need you to stay with me. I know you're contracting right now and it's hurting like hell, but I need you to hold your head back, so we can get control of this nosebleed. And you need to calm down, so your blood pressure doesn't skyrocket," Tangie said as she kneeled down beside me.

"Can . . . someone . . . please . . . call . . . my . . . mama?" I managed to get out between breaths.

"I think your sister already did," Tangie replied.

I looked to my left and saw Niecey pacing the floor with the phone glued to her ear, while Toby was in a corner, having what seemed like a heated conversation with Jerome.

"Did . . . Lil Ray . . . come back . . . yet?" I asked.

Tangie looked at me for a quick second, smiled sheepishly, then turned her attention toward the EMTs rushing into the lounge. I didn't know what that was about, but by that look on her face, I could tell that the answer was no. While Tangie briefed the paramedics on my condition and my mind drifted off to Lil Ray, another contraction hit me a lot harder than the first and had me doubling over in more pain.

"Breathe, LaLa! Breathe," I heard someone shout.

"How can I breathe?" I yelled back. "With your hand and this towel covering my face, it's kind of hard for me to do that shit."

I didn't mean to snap at the young woman like that, but when everything that had preceded this moment started to flash before my eyes, I got mad all over again. Mya was foul as hell for blurting that shit out like that. I couldn't wait until I dropped this baby. I had something really special for her ass, and couldn't nobody on God's green earth save her from it. Not only had she screwed up JaNair's special moment, but she had probably destroyed any hope of my and Jay's friendship ever being restored too. I had known that bitch was up to something the minute I'd seen her ease her ho ass into the VIP section. I should've said something then, but I'd refrained.

"What the fuck is she doing up here?"

"Who you talkin' 'bout?" Lil Ray asked before he took another sip of his drink.

"Mya's trifling and thirsty ass. She looks like she's up to something too."

Lil Ray laughed. "How can you tell that? From what I see, she's up here just like we are, celebrating her cousin's birthday."

"Nigga, when was the last time you saw Jay and Mya together?"

He thought about it for a second, then shrugged his shoulders.

"See? That's what I'm talking about. I don't even think JaNair invited her to this party, either, so why is she here?"

"You females kill me. Let that girl enjoy herself. Look, it's obvious Jay ain't tripping, or she wouldn't be talking to her right now."

He nodded his head in their direction, and sure enough, the distant cousins were having some kind of awkward-looking conversation. I watched as both Mya and JaNair put on their fakest smiles and exchanged pleasantries. Their interaction looked so forced and fake, I could only imagine what they were saying to one another.

Yeah, that bitch is up to something, *I thought to myself as I watched Mya's gaze slide over to Jerome's every few seconds.*

Twenty minutes, five songs, and two cranberry juices later, the waitresses in the lounge finally brought out JaNair's lavish cake. My stomach, which had started to hurt after all the different foods we ate, was now feeling a bit queasy. I was so ready for this night to end, so that I could go home and lie down.

"Are you okay?" Lil Ray asked as I grabbed my stomach and his shoulder at the same time. As a sharp pain shot through my belly, I gave a quick smile and a head nod, just to avert any type of panic from him.

A few minutes later, another pain shot through my back, and it had my knees buckling a bit. When Lil Ray looked at me again with concern etched across his face, I mustered up all the strength that I could and acted as if everything was still okay. I knew I should've said something then, but I wanted to see JaNair's face when she got her big surprise.

Jerome going down on one knee, with a small black velvet box in his hand, had everyone in the VIP gasping at the same time. The look on JaNair's face was indescribable, and I couldn't tell whether she was shocked or annoyed. When I followed her line of sight and saw the expression on Mya's face, I just knew some shit was about to pop off.

Even though we were mad at each other and hadn't talked to one another in a minute, that twin telepathy thing Niecey and I sometimes had must've kicked in.

Either that or she must've noticed what was about to happen, because she and Toby came and stood next to me.

When JaNair started to question Mya about the look on her face, I just knew Mya was about to tell Jay about her and Jerome fucking around. But when I heard her say, "Jerome fucking your so-called best friend and possibly getting her pregnant," I could feel all the color drain from my face as the pressure that was building up at the bottom of my stomach suddenly got released and the contents of my stomach spilled all down my legs.

I reached out for Lil Ray after Mya revealed my dirty little secret, but was met with a scowl and him shrugging his arm from my hold. Not even bothering to look back, he stormed out of the VIP section.

"Ray . . . RayShaun!" I cried out, only to be ignored.

"LaNiece, we were able to stop the nosebleed, but now we need to get you to the hospital," the young paramedic said, breaking me from my thoughts.

"Hospital? But why?"

She looked around at everyone standing around me. "Um, we need to take you to the hospital because your water broke and it seems like this baby wants to come out tonight."

"*What!*" I yelled at the top of my lungs. "It's too early. I have two more months to go." I was becoming scared now. I didn't have anyone by my side, and I didn't want my baby to be premature.

"That's why we're on our way to the hospital now. We've already called your doctor and informed him about what's going on. He's already in the delivery ward, waiting for your arrival."

I didn't know what to say or how to feel after that. Lil Ray was nowhere to be found, and I even managed to lose sight of Niecey and Toby as the EMTs pushed me through the lounge, out the front door, and into the ambulance that was waiting for me outside.

The ride to the hospital was short, and we got there within fifteen minutes. When we got to the room that I would be delivering in, the first familiar face I saw was my mother's. JaNair was supposed to be the second person I allowed to witness the birth, but we all knew that wouldn't be happening anytime soon. I was so happy that I finally had someone there with me that I started to cry while the doctors and nurses stood around me, telling me to push.

After being in labor for twelve hours straight, I finally gave birth to my beautiful brown-eyed, curly-haired, caramel-colored princess. Weighing four pounds, one ounce, and measuring eighteen inches long, my little angel was the most adorable baby I'd ever seen. Due to a case of thrush, she stayed in the NICU for three days, but after it cleared up, she was by my side day and night.

"Ah, LaLa, my grandbaby is beautiful," my mom said as I nursed my bundle of joy. "What are you going to name her?"

"I was thinking—" I began, but I was interrupted by the door to my room being pushed open.

Shock instantly covered my face as Lil Ray walked in, smelling like a goddamn weed dispensary. Before I could even get into his ass, the door opened once again and Niecey, Toby, and a distraught Jerome walked in.

My baby must've sensed my mood change, because as soon as the door closed, she started to cry at the top of her lungs. With every eye now on me, I tried to calm her down any way I could. I bounced her, swung her, patted her back, checked her diaper, and even tried to feed her again, but nothing seemed to be working.

Finally, Niecey stepped forward, with a tear-streaked face, and said, "Let me hold her for a minute."

Seeing the tears fall from her eyes had a few tears start to fall from mine. I didn't know if this was her way of forgiving me for what had happened, but I'd take whatever I could to have my and my sister's relationship back to the way it was. We looked at each other and nodded our heads at the same time, silently agreeing to put our differences aside for the time being. When Niecey walked closer to me and was in a comfortable standing position, I gently placed my baby in her arms. It was just that fast that my love baby started to quiet down, and soon she fell asleep.

"I guess my niece likes me a little better than her own mama, huh?" Niecey joked, which caused everyone to chuckle a bit, including Jerome.

"So what are you going to name her?" Toby asked as he stood behind Niecey and smiled down at the sight before him.

I was just about to answer his question when the door to my room swung open again.

"Oh, I'm sorry, you guys, but there are way too many people in the room right now. That's not healthy for the little beauty you got there in your arms," said the nurse who was assigned to my room. "How about Granny and the proud father stay for right now? Then, after fifteen minutes or so, the next round can come in."

I didn't know why, but her mentioning the proud father had me dropping my head down in embarrassment.

Jerome, who had been sulking in the corner, cleared his throat and spoke up. "Unfortunately, it would be kind of hard for us to decipher who the child belongs to, seeing as we have two possible fathers in the room."

The nurse scrunched up her eyebrows, then looked from me to Jerome, then to Lil Ray. I didn't know if she had crossed out Toby because he was white or because he was standing close to Niecey, but she never glanced his way.

"Okay . . . I see. Well, if you want, I can go get two DNA kits so we can clear up this whole thing about the baby's paternity."

We all shook our heads in agreement just as there was a knock on the door, followed by the sound of a familiar voice. Big Will pushed the door open and strolled into the room.

"Excuse me, ma'am, but do you mind making that three DNA tests? I need one, too, since LaLa here slept with me and these two other niggas around the time of conception." Big Will said. Then, to add insult to injury, he added, "Oh, and by the way, can you please make sure it's the rapid one? I don't wanna be here any longer than I have to."

The shocked look on the nurse's face and everyone else's was priceless. The only thing I could think of as I sank deeper into this hospital bed while pulling the sheet over my head was, *Shit!*

Jerome

I watched JaNair as she walked out of my club and possibly out of my life for the last time. The crowd that was around us had dispersed. Everyone was in their own cliques and was either talking about everything that had just happened or enjoying the free bottles of alcohol a couple of the waitresses had just brought up.

I scanned the crowd for Mya's ass, but she was nowhere to be found. I couldn't believe she had told JaNair about me and LaLa, even after I had given her trifling ass that two thousand dollars. I couldn't wait to catch up with her; she was going to wish she had never fucked with me in her life.

"Hey, Jerome. Are you okay?" I heard a soft voice ask from behind me.

I turned around and came face-to-face with Tangie. A look of genuine concern was etched across her face. I nodded my head in response to her question, just to have her reach up and smack me in the back of it.

"How could you be so stupid, Jerome? Her best friend? You had me going to her house and putting in good words for you when you knew all along that LaLa was carrying your baby. You didn't think this would get out?"

"It wouldn't have if Mya had kept her mouth shut," I mumbled.

Tangie looked at me for a minute, as if she was seeing everything that was replaying in my mind about the past few months. I normally was very hard to intimidate, but her stare was doing something to me.

"What?" I finally asked as I looked at anything but her.
"You fucked her, too, didn't you?"

"Wh-what? Fucked who too? You tripping, Tang.
Everybody in this club knows I fucked LaLa, and that's it."

She walked up closer to me with her hands on her hip,
getting in my personal space. "I'm not talking about LaLa,
Jerome. I'm talking about Mya. It all makes sense now.
I was wondering why she was looking at JaNair like she
wanted to strangle her the whole time you were trying to
propose to her. I don't even know if I could describe that
look on her face as jealousy. It was more like . . . like . . .
malice." She shook her head. "Jerome, how could you be
so stupid? I'm quite sure your relationship with JaNair
is pretty fucked up now, but just in case it isn't, once she
finds out that you fucked her cousin too, your chances of
getting her back will be pretty nonexistent."

I turned my back to her and looked out at the crowd.
Everyone was still dancing and having a good time. My
hands were clutching the railing so hard that I could feel
the square edges of the banister indenting my palms. I
didn't want to hear that shit Tangie was saying, even
though it was the truth. JaNair belonged to me, and she
always would. I'd be damned if I let this little mishap
in our relationship stop us from being together. I loved
JaNair. Shit, I was in love with her, and I might have a
funny way of showing it, but I'd do anything to get her
back, even if that meant getting rid of Mya's bitch ass,
so that what she and I did would never come to light. I
didn't have to worry about LaLa saying anything, especially if she wanted me to be in my supposed baby's life.

Speaking of LaLa, I wondered how fast we could get
this DNA test done. I had seen her dramatic ass when
she'd fallen to the floor in pain. She had looked at me for
a brief minute, and I didn't know why. I hoped she didn't
think I was going to be by her side while she was going
into labor. Her ass was really crazy if she thought that.

I guess Tangie must've got tired of waiting for me to turn back around, because when I finally did, she was no longer standing there. Low key, I was kind of glad too, because I didn't really feel like hearing her mouth anymore. I made my way through the crowd, hoping that JaNair would pop up somewhere. I knew that was wishful thinking, but a nigga needed to have at least a little glimmer of hope. I was on my way to my office but changed my mind in mid-stride. I really needed a drink, so I headed over to the bar. All we had up in the VIP was that weak-ass moscato champagne JaNair liked, and I was in dire need of something much stronger.

"What can I get for you, boss man?" asked the new bartender, Whitney, as she wiped down the already clean counter in front of me.

"Get me a shot . . . No, make that a double shot of Jack on ice and keep 'em coming."

She looked at me for a minute before she started to make my drink. "Night not going so well for you, huh?"

I took the full shot glass she had just placed in front of me, and downed the brown liquid in one quick swoop. "Give me another one. And what you just said would be an understatement. My night was horrific, and I don't have anyone to blame but myself."

She sat the next double in front of me, and I drank that as fast as I did the first. My chest was burning, and I was going to have a hell of a hangover in the morning, but I didn't give a fuck. I needed to be somewhere other than where I was right now.

Whitney placed the third round of my drink of choice in front of me without me having to ask. She then turned around and started to fill an order for a few people that had just walked up to the bar. I took my phone out of my pocket and dialed JaNair's number. My call went straight to voicemail, and I wasn't the least bit surprised when her voicemail kept picking up every time I hit REDIAL.

ShaNiece

"So what do you want to do, babe? I'm down for whatever you choose. We can head home or head to the hospital. It's your choice," Toby said.

We were standing outside the club, watching the ambulance that LaLa was in pull off. A part of me wanted to go to the hospital to be by my twin's side, but the other part was still mad at her for betraying me like she did.

I called my mother and told her what was happening, so I knew she'd be at the hospital before LaLa's ambulance even arrived. When I tried to call Lil Ray's phone, it just rang and rang before the voicemail finally picked up. I left him a message. Hopefully, he would get out of his feelings and make it to the hospital in time to see the baby being born. She could possibly be his, and I knew he would really hate himself if he missed the birth.

The blowing wind caused a chill to run through my body, which had goose bumps running up and down my arms. The short black sequin dress I had on did nothing to keep me warm or get me close to it. With my arms crossed over my chest and my hands moving up and down, I stared into the darkness at the end of the street, stuck. I didn't know why I couldn't move from the spot I was standing in. It was as if my feet were planted in the ground as I contemplated what my next move was going to be.

"Niecey, let's leave or go back into the club, babe. You're freezing, and I left our jackets in the car," I heard

Toby say into my ear after he walked up behind me and wrapped his arms around my waist. "If you don't want to be bothered with anybody, we can go into my office and just chill there until you decide what you want to do." The kiss he placed on my shoulder warmed me up a bit, but I was still shivering a little.

"Can we just go? I don't feel like going to the hospital, home, or back inside the club right now. Can we go to your place instead?"

"You don't even have to ask, Niecey. You know I like having you there."

I smiled and watched as Toby went to retrieve his car from the valet. I didn't know why he never let any of the workers park or fetch his car. Wasn't that their job?

I felt my phone vibrating in my purse and took it out. I had a few missed calls from my mother, while the rest were from Will. Since I wasn't sure how quickly Toby would appear with the car, instead of calling Will back, I sent him a text.

Me: What do you want, Will?

Will: You!

Me: That's funny, seeing as my sister is in the hospital, about to have your baby. I was thinking it was her you wanted.

I stood waiting for Will to text me back for about two minutes, but when no text arrived, I put my phone back in my purse. As I continued to wait on Toby, some guy approached me.

"Hey, baby. You know you're way too fine to be all hugged up with that white dude. A beautiful queen such as yourself needs to be with a strong black king such as myself," he declared. "Why don't you come back over to our side of town and let me show you what you've been missing?"

I looked at this idiot and rolled my eyes. Men could be so stupid sometimes. *You mad that I'm with a white man because of what?* I thought. Niggas killed me. They had so much to say and wanted to be in their feelings when they saw you with another race, but they treated you like shit when they had you. I shook my head. This shit wad crazy.

Seconds later, Toby pulled up to the front of the club in his smoke-gray Jaguar XK and hopped out of the car to open the passenger door for me. Before I got in, I heard the same dude who had just tried to talk to me say to his friends, "Oh, she got her a rich white dude, so that bitch ain't never coming back."

They all shared a laugh, which was fine with me, and to show them just how fine it was, I grabbed Toby by the back of the head and pulled his lips down to mine. I kissed him with everything I had in me, and he did the same. When I wrapped my arms around his neck, I felt him slip his arms around my waist, then palm my ass. As he drew me to him, I kept teetering on my tippy-toes. It was like he wanted to lift me up, but then he would change his mind. We must've been there for a minute, savoring the taste of each other's tongues, before a loud honk of the horn from the car behind his broke our connection. I pulled back first and looked up at Toby, whose eyes were still closed. When he opened them, I felt my panties, which were already wet, become drenched.

"What was that about?" he asked in a husky voice. His eyes were hooded and low, as if he had just finished smoking some of Cali's finest.

"I just wanted to say thank you for being there and always showing me a good time."

He licked his lips. "You're welcome, babe. Now let's get out of here before I have to fire one of these fools for being so rude to their boss and his lady."

His lady. I kind of liked the sound of that, although I still had a few reservations. What ole boy had said about me being a queen in need of a strong black king had me in my thoughts. Was I really ready to go through everything Toby and I would go through as an interracial couple? Was I ready to be in another relationship so soon? Was I really over Will? I knew I'd forgiven him before, such as when he'd had sex with other girls during our off time, but could I forgive him for fucking my sister?

A lot of questions started to run through my mind about my future, and I was unsure about a lot of things, except for one. I balled up my fist and instantly got a headache when my mind drifted over to my ex-best friend. Her ass better be glad Toby had held me back earlier. Whenever I caught up to that bitch Mya, she was going to get her ass beat. I may not be on good terms with my sister right now, but what Mya did to her tonight was low down and dirty. Her ass got something coming soon, and if I were her, I'd lay low for as long as I could.

Toby opening the passenger-side door broke me from my train of thought. I knew the scowl on my face was pretty evident, and I tried to hide it before he got a chance to ask me what was wrong. I got into the car, and he closed the door for me, then walked off toward the valet booth. After he went over to the impatient worker and had a few choice words with him, he finally hopped in the car and pulled off. I looked over at him and smiled as he laced our hands together and kissed the back of mine. Toby was indeed one of the finest men I'd seen, and so far he'd done everything right. I wondered whether he would be able to hold me down when shit started to get a little rocky, or would he jump ship and go find a snow bunny to occupy his time?

Jerome

I looked down at my ringing phone, hoping it was JaNair finally calling me back, but to my utter disappointment, it was LaLa's number that was flashing across my screen again. I ignored this call, like I had the others for the past couple of hours. I didn't want to talk to her or to anybody who wasn't JaNair right now.

I was still sitting at the bar, drinking shot after shot of whiskey, trying to drown all my sorrows with alcohol. Whitney had already gone home for the night, and I was glad about that. She was a little too bold and aggressive, if you ask me. While sitting there, drinking my life away, I had told her about everything that had been happening to me, from meeting and falling in love with JaNair, to lying to her about my son, to fucking her cousin and best friend, who had probably been delivering my baby as we spoke.

Whitney had given me her little take on the situation, which was her bad-mouthing JaNair and saying how she had to know that I was cheating on her. Something about a woman's intuition. Then she had said that JaNair probably didn't really care about me fucking other bitches, because she was fucking another nigga herself. She had said all that before turning around and asking me if I wanted to come to her house tonight or if I wanted to take her up to my office so we could talk in private.

The old Jerome probably would've jumped on the offer. Whitney was bad as hell—average height, brown skin, thick as fuck, with a pretty face and a banging-ass body—but for some reason, I hadn't been able to do it. She'd offered the pussy to me on a silver platter, and I hadn't cared. My dick hadn't even jumped when she'd accidentally brushed her titties across my hand as it hung over the bar. I already had enough going on with LaLa and Mya's ass, and I didn't want to complicate things any further. I laughed at myself now. Where was all this damn self-control when I was fucking with their asses?

I didn't believe the shit Whitney had said about JaNair cheating on me one bit, but then again, that nappy-headed nigga from next door kept popping into my head. Had she been fucking that nigga this whole time? Was she with him right now? I wondered. I had called her phone so much that I had actually used up all the battery on mine. My phone was now dead and was charging behind the bar, on Whitney's charger. Her shift had ended about thirty minutes ago, and when I'd gone to take my phone off her charger, she'd told me to just keep it and leave it behind the bar when I was done charging. She'd get it when she came in for her shift later on that night. Now it was just me and Raul, another bartender who worked for me at the bar, and he was still serving me drinks.

I gazed out at the dwindling crowd, then looked at my watch. It was almost closing time, and people were still sitting around, lounging and having a good time. I thought about closing up early, but I changed my mind when I saw that people were still dropping bills for bottle service. Although the money was good, I was still ready for everyone to leave so that I could head on over to JaNair's house as soon as possible. I knew I'd said that I'd give it a week, but I had changed my mind. I needed to see her and plead my case to her as soon as possible if there was any chance of us saving our relationship.

Before my phone had died, I'd seen that I had a few missed calls from a couple of people. Toby had texted me earlier saying that he was on his way to take Niecey home and that he would be back after he had dropped her off. I had told him to go on and stay with her for the night and had assured him that we could do the books and everything else that needed to be done tomorrow afternoon. Gerald and his girl must've dipped out when everyone else did, because I hadn't seen him since JaNair smacked the shit out of me. One of the missed calls was from him, but I'd decided to call him back later. I hadn't felt like hearing any of his lectures at that moment, anyway.

"All right, Mr. Hayes. I'm about to do last call. Did you want another shot before I start to clean up the bar?"

"Yeah, Raul. Go ahead and pour me two more double shots. Call the back and tell Manny and the rest of them not to take any more orders and to start getting everything cleaned up back there. I want everything to be shut down and wiped down within the next hour, okay?"

He nodded his head and picked up the phone receiver hanging on the wall to deliver the message.

I swallowed both shots and stood up. For a minute, it felt as if everything around me was spinning, but I shook it off and walked around the bar to retrieve my phone. When it finally powered up, I got a little excited to see my notification light going off. I was hoping and praying that JaNair had at least texted me back with a "Fuck you!" or something. I'd even be content with a voicemail telling me to fuck off. I just needed some form of communication from her so that I would know that not all hope was lost.

Hell, who am I kidding? I thought. I'd be surprised if she didn't block my number before the night was over. I dialed her number a few more times, and like the thousand times before, I kept getting her voicemail. Unlike all the other times, though, I decided to try my luck and leave a message this time.

"Hey, JaNair. I know I'm the last person you want to hear from right now, baby, but I just wanted to let you know that I am so sorry about everything that happened tonight. Believe me when I say that I only wanted to make your birthday night something special." I laughed. "It was special, all right, just not the type of special I wanted you to have. Look, I know you don't want to see me right now or anything, but that's still not going to stop me from coming by the house tomorrow. If you're there, please answer the door so we can talk about this.

"JaNair, please believe me when I say that I do love you, and I didn't mean for any of this to happen. What LaLa and I did means nothing and meant nothing to me. If it helps, I don't even think the baby is mine, because we used a condom every time we had sex." I cursed at myself for just revealing that LaLa and I had had sex more than once, but oh well . . . I'd rather get it all out in the open right now. "Anyways, babe, when you get this message, please call me back. If not, I'll hopefully see you when I stop by sometime tomorrow. I love you, JaNair, and I plan on showing you how sorry I am, if I have to spend the rest of my life doing so. I love you, babe. Bye."

I ended the call after I left my message, and tucked my phone into my pocket. I knew she wouldn't call me back, but at least she'd get the message.

Almost an hour and a half later, the lounge was closed, and everyone but Raul and the cleaning service was gone. After collecting all the money and receipts from the registers, I went to my office and deposited the night's earnings in the safe. Normally, I'd count up all the cash, then tie a rubber band around it, with the amount recorded on a little note. My head was spinning so much from all the drinking that I couldn't even think straight.

I was lying on my leather couch with my eyes closed and my arm over my face when a light tapping on the door drew my attention.

"Yeah?" I called, slurring. I wasn't sure if I had spoken loudly enough for whoever was on the other side of the door to hear.

"Uh, Mr. Hayes? It's Raul. The cleaning crew is done, and I'm about to head out too. Was there anything else that you needed?"

I must've dozed off for a minute, because when I opened my eyes and sat up, Raul was standing over me, with a look of concern on his face.

"Are you okay, Mr. Hayes? You did have a lot to drink. Do you need me to call a cab for you?"

Without answering, I just waved him off and stood up. I wobbled for a second but got my bearings. We left my office together, and when we walked out to the main floor, I saw that the cleaning crew had already gone and had left their invoice on one of the tables by the front door.

"Okay, Raul. See you tomorrow."

"You're not leaving?"

"Naw. I have some things to take care of before I go," I replied as we walked to the front door. "You be safe, though, all right?" I added as he stepped outside.

I didn't even give him a chance to respond before I closed the door in his face and locked all the locks.

Instead of going through the kitchen to check the back door, which I was sure Manny had already locked, I headed straight to the bar to get myself another drink.

"Johnnie Walker Black! Haven't hung with you in a while," I said aloud to myself before I unscrewed the top on my libation of choice and drank straight from the bottle.

I see that it is going to be a long night for me. I'm just glad I have some great company to keep me entertained, I thought.

JaNair

"Aye, you hit my line. Leave me a message after the beep and I'll get back to you as soon as I can . . ."

Beep.

I hung up my cell, utterly frustrated. Semaj's phone was still going straight to voicemail, and I didn't know any other way to contact him. I thought about calling up to the Rap-A-Lot office and seeing if someone could *patch* me through to him, but I doubted that this would go the way I wanted.

I had just gotten off the plane from Los Angeles and was now standing in the middle of the Dallas/Fort Worth International Airport, looking like a lost puppy.

"Maybe this wasn't such a good idea," I said to no one in particular.

"Why you say that?" I heard someone say behind me.

When I turned around, a short, stubby, brown-skinned girl with some big-ass hips and a big-ass booty was standing behind me. She had on some black jeans that were a size too small for her. The white shirt that she had on left nothing to the imagination when it came to her cleavage. Her jet-black hair with blue tips was in a cute bob that framed her chubby face. The style looked good on her. However, the oversize glasses, which kept sliding down her nose, and the four gold teeth she proudly displayed as she smiled at me were a bit much.

"I'm sorry. I was talking out loud to myself. I wasn't expecting anyone to respond to me."

"Gal, you so crazy." Her Southern accent was thick as hell. "Where you from?"

"Uhhh . . ." I wasn't too sure if I wanted to divulge that type of information to this stranger. Although she seemed nice and everything, I didn't know this chick from a can of paint.

"It's okay. I already know who you are and where you from. I just wanted to make sure I had the right gal." She took out her phone and looked at something on her screen, then looked back at me. "Boss boy wasn't lying. You are one pretty gal."

"Boss boy?"

She laughed. "I'm sorry, honey. You probably think I'm all kinds of crazy right now. Let's start from the beginning." She opened up the big black folder in her hand, then shuffled around some papers until she found the one she was looking for and pulled it out. "Are you Ja . . . ?"

"JaNair!"

"Yes. JaNair Livingston?"

"Maybe. It depends on who wants to know." What was there for me to lose right now? Her knowing my name had to mean something.

"Well, I'm Earlnesha, but you can call me Neesh," she said proudly as she stretched out her hand for me to shake. "And I'm here to pick you up and take you to your destination."

"Which would be where?"

"To Mr. Jones, of course. He's been real busy in the studio, trying to get this album finished, so he couldn't come pick you up himself."

See, now I was a little confused. How could Semaj know that I would be here? He hadn't answered his phone since I'd left my party. And no one knew about the ticket except for me and . . . I shook my head. Ms. Shirley or Lil Ray. It had to be one of the two. They were the only ones that knew about my gift, and seeing as Lil Ray had had a front-row seat to the shenanigans that went on last night, it was probably he who had got in touch with Semaj and given him the heads-up. But what would make Semaj think that I was headed this way?

"I'm sorry, Ms. Livingston . . . ," Neesh said, breaking my train of thought.

"Please don't call me that. My mother is in Florida, living it up with the dolphins and shit. Just call me JaNair or Jay."

She nodded her head and smiled, gold teeth shining like new money. "Okay, Jay. Are you ready to go?"

I wanted to ask her where we were going, but seeing that she was connected with *Mr. Jones* in some way, I was pretty sure we would be heading to him.

"Do you need to get your things from baggage claim?" she asked.

I shook my head no.

"Well, are you hungry?"

"I could eat something."

"Well, while we're still in Dallas, we can stop by Jonathan's and get some breakfast. I know you from California and all, so I hope you not one of them carb-counting freaks," she said as she looked me up and down. I still had on my gold dress and heels from my party. I should've gone home and changed, but I had been so ready to go. The little jacket I had on covered up my exposed back, but it didn't hide anything else. My slim waist, thick thighs, and full hips were on full display. There was no sign of carb counting on this body.

"No, I'm not. I eat a little bit of everything. Probably eat more than you." I knew that that was a little bit of shade, but I had to get her back for what she had just said.

"Humph. If you ask me, you need to eat a little more of something. You a thick one, but not as thick as they like 'em down here. The BBW movement is taking over, gal, and Mr. Jones been down here long enough to jump on it. I hope your feelings don't get hurt when that sexy dread-head muthafucka starts checking for me." She laughed, and so did I.

"Well, if that's the case, may the best woman win."

She nodded her head. "I like you, Jay. Even though I've known you for only a few minutes now, you seem like real cool people. Plus, Mr. Jones is always talking about you, so it seems like I know you already."

That little bit of information had me blush slightly on the inside. Semaj must've been talking about me a lot to make her feel that way. It seemed like it had been forever since we last saw each other or talked, and I couldn't wait to see him.

We made it to Jonathan's in about thirty minutes. By the time we got there, my stomach was roaring from my being so hungry. Neesh recommended the fried chicken and waffles, so that was what I ordered, along with a side of eggs and grits, and sweet tea. After we had finished cleaning our plates, we sat and chopped it up for a minute about our personal lives and how she had come to be Semaj's assistant.

"My daddy got tired of paying for my things and told me I needed to get a job if I wanted to keep maintaining my lifestyle. He said that I would start by having to pay half of everything—my rent, car note, insurance, and so on. Said if I didn't find a job within a month, he'd cut me off. After trying for three weeks straight, I finally broke down and asked Daddy if he had a position in the record company that I could fill. Since I didn't have any *real work* experience, he asked if I would be willing to be an assistant to one of his new producers. At first I said no, because I was not about to fetch another grown-ass person's coffee and shit, but once I saw Mr. Jones fine ass that day when I came up to a session, I changed my tone real fast. I came to work the first day with a steaming hot cup of coffee for him in one hand and a bag of bagels in the other."

She laughed as we both stood up from the table. "Now, I ain't gon lie to you, Jay. I tried to push up on him on a few different occasions, but he turned me down every time, so I fell back. However, I can't say the same about the other bitches that work there and live here." We headed outside, and she pointed in the direction of our ride. Our driver was waiting patiently behind the wheel.

"Yeah . . . I bet you can't," I mumbled as we walked to the truck.

I hopped into the back of the truck and closed the door. These bitches in Texas really had another thing coming if they thought I was just gonna sit back and let them take what would be mine.

ShaNiece

"I don't want to hear that shit, ShaNiece. At the end of the day, LaNiece is still your twin sister, your other half, and no matter how hard you wish she wasn't right now, she still is."

"Okay. I hear you, Mom," I sighed into the phone.

"I know you hear me, but do you understand?"

I nodded my head no but told her yes with my mouth.

"Well, now that we're all on the same page, you need to get your ass on up here to see your new niece. Make sure you text Will and tell his bitch ass to get up here too. Lil Ray should be here by now, and make sure you have Toby call Jerome so that he can be here as well. I already told LaLa there was no need in prolonging this here situation. We need to do this test today so that the right man can sign the birth certificate and be in his child's life."

I silently agreed, then ended the call with my mother. Even after that thirty-minute conversation we had just had, I still didn't want to go to the hospital. For some reason, it was really starting to fuck with my train of thought that my twin sister could've just given birth to my ex's baby. Not only was Will my ex, but he was also my first love, the first boy I had ever kissed, the first boy I had ever had sex with, and also the first boy ever to break my heart. In between our "breakup" stints, I had met and messed with a few other dudes, but that had never changed the way I felt about him or what he meant to me.

Looking over at a napping Toby, I knew I shouldn't be feeling some type of way about the situation, but I was. Yeah, Toby was showing me a lot of things that Will probably never could . . . but still.

It was at times like this that I wished I really had someone to talk to. Since I'd been betrayed by my sister and I'd finally seen Mya for the ho that she was, I didn't have anyone.

I picked up my phone and scrolled down my contact list until I came to Will's name. I thought about giving him a call but then decided against it and sent him a text instead.

Me: Your presence is needed at the hospital as soon as you get a minute.

It took about two minutes, but he finally responded.

Will: Why? What's the matter? Are you okay?

Me: My well-being isn't any of your concern anymore.

Will: Why not? Regardless of what you think, Niecey, I still care about you, and I always will.

Pssst. This nigga. Muthafuckas always wanna say the right things when they know you have moved on. I wasn't falling for that shit this time around. Will and I would never be together, even if the baby turned out not to be his.

Me: Thank you for caring, but it's not needed. Just make sure you make your way down to the hospital for the DNA test today. Your maybe baby was born sometime this morning.

After ten minutes had passed with no response, I put my phone down on the coffee table and went to join Toby on his comfy couch. I was going to go see about my niece, but not until after I had had a few hours of sleep and had got ahold of that fuck nigga Jerome.

As soon as I lay down in front of Toby, he wrapped his strong arm around my waist and pulled me closer to his body. The arm that he'd used to prop his head up was now curled around my neck, giving his lips complete access to the open yet sensitive area.

He placed his nose against my skin and inhaled my scent. "You always smell so good, baby. I will never get used to the way your essence intoxicates me."

"Is that right?" I asked as I turned in his embrace to face him.

Eyes still closed, he bit his bottom lip and slowly nodded his head. "Why do you think I'm always hugging on you and shit? It's like I can't stop."

I laughed and lightly slapped him on his arm. When my hand started to caress his bicep, he opened his eyes, which I noticed were filled with lust, and just looked at me. The magnetic pull that we seemed to always have whenever we looked at each other didn't skip a beat and had us moving closer to one another. As soon as his lips touched mine, my body was on fire.

Hands down, Toby was the best kisser I'd ever experienced. His kiss was never sloppy, nor was it too refined. It was both sensitive and bold, and romantic and horny, at the same time. His tongue was just like him: adventurous and soft and ready to explore the unknown. I swear one simple peck from him touched my whole body every time, and I just couldn't get enough.

"Why you always trying to start something with those drugging kisses you give me?" he asked as he pulled back from our connection.

I blushed. "You need to be asking yourself that same question."

"I'm saying, though . . . I don't know what I'm going to do with you. You're starting to become one of my favorite pastimes. The little time that we do spend together now is starting to not be enough for me." He placed his finger under my chin and lifted it up, making sure I would pay attention to whatever he was about to say. "Niecey, I know this may be too soon for you, but what do you think about mov—"

At that moment, my phone started to go off. By the ringtone, I could tell that it was a text message, but he didn't know that. I hopped off the couch and picked up my phone, then mouthed to him that I'd be back. I knew that was a bitch move, seeing as he was about to ask me to move in with him, but I didn't think that I was ready for all of that.

Toby was probably the best thing for me right now, but I was still dealing with some things that might affect our relationship in the future. It wouldn't be fair for me to get involved with him when I was still in my feelings about the way Will did me. Before I decided to start a new life with someone else, I needed to end the one with the person I had before.

Looking down at my phone, I wasn't surprised to see that the text message was from Will. What I wasn't expecting was what he had to say.

Will: ShaNiece, I am truly sorry for all the hurt and pain that I've caused you in the years that we have been together. You know as well as I do that you are my heart and I can't live without you. I know that white boy is occupying your time right now, but he'll never occupy your mind, body, and soul like I did. We've both done wrong in our past, and we managed to get over it. This little thing with your sister should be no different. I know in my heart that the baby isn't mine. You are the only one I want to carry my kids. Let's meet up whenever you get a minute so we can talk. I love you, babe. No one will ever change that. . . .

See what I'm talking about? I know I said all that shit earlier, but with messages like this, why wouldn't I be confused about what I wanted to do?

***

We were on the 105, headed to the Lotus Bomb to pick up Jerome. After I had talked to Will by text for a few minutes, I'd gone back into the living room and asked Toby if he could locate his dog of a friend.

He had called Jerome's phone the whole night, had even gone over to his house to check on him, but he hadn't been there. About an hour ago he'd got a phone call from one of his employees, telling him that they had found Jerome's dumb ass passed out drunk on the kitchen floor. He'd said the nigga had trashed the majority of the food they had in the fridge for tonight's menu and had broken a gang of plates and wineglasses.

"I knew I shouldn't have left that muthafucka alone last night. Even though he looked like he was okay, I knew his ass really wasn't." Toby was on the phone as he drove. I assumed he was speaking with their mutual friend Gerald, who was also en route to the lounge.

"Man, I don't know. But he can't be mad at nobody but himself, since this is all that nigga's fault. We both told him to stop messing with that girl, but he wouldn't listen. Naw. I don't think she found out about that."

Found out about what? I wondered.

"Hell yeah, JaNair really would've been tripping then. All right, man, I'm almost there. I'll see you when we pull up." Toby laughed, then looked at me. "Yeah, *we*, man. Me and Niecey." He laughed again. "I ain't gotta tell you shit, bruh. All right, though. Talk to you in a minute. Later."

I smirked. "What was that last part of your conversation about?"

"You already know it was about you."

"Yeah, but what about me?"

He laughed. "That's for me to know and for you to mind your own business. I didn't say anything when you got up and ran to the bathroom to answer that mystery call you got."

I smacked my lips and looked out the window. I didn't want him to see the shocked look on my face. I wasn't expecting him to snap back with that.

"It was not a mystery call," I finally said. "I just had to use the bathroom at the same time that my phone went off."

He gave me a "Yeah, right" look, then focused his attention back on the open road. I didn't know why I felt the need to lie. It wasn't like I was *with* him. I guessed I just didn't want to see a look of disappointment cross his face once I told him that I was talking to Will and making plans to meet up with him. I had told Toby all about my past relationship with him. The good, the bad, and the ugly. All he'd said once I had finished my story was that I deserved better and that I was worth way more than what I gave myself credit for.

When we arrived at the Lotus Bomb, there were a couple of cars in the back, where Toby usually parked. One I recognized as Jerome's; the other was a nice-ass Range Rover that I'd never seen before.

We walked in the open back door, in search of fuck boy, but we didn't find him anywhere in the kitchen or the main room. When we walked to the back, where the offices were, I could see Jerome in his office. He was lying on the couch, with a tall brown-skinned dude, a short light-skinned girl, and the Mexican dude that worked at the bar standing over him.

"Man, Jerome, get your ass up! You got me out here early in the morning with my girl and shit, when I can be at home, eating a breakfast fit for a king."

Jerome slurred something I couldn't make out, then turned on his side and threw up in the trash bucket that was sitting next to him.

"Aw, hell naw, babe. You know I do not have the stomach for this. I'ma be in the car, waiting for you, okay?" the light-skinned girl said as she patted her man on the arm. Then she turned around to walk out of the office and came face-to-face with Toby and me. "Oh, hey, Toby!" She looked at me. "I know G should be glad you're here. That nigga is really wasted." She turned her attention back toward me and held out her hand. "Hi. I'm Zadaya. It's nice to finally meet the woman Toby can't stop talking about."

Was Toby blushing? I really couldn't tell, because as soon as I looked at him, he turned his face. Aw, he *was* blushing. *How cute.*

After I introduced myself to Zadaya and promised to meet up for drinks sometime, she left us, her man, and a throwing-up Jerome in the office.

"Yo, G, what's good?" Toby said to Gerald. They slapped hands.

"I don't know, Toby. I just know I got a phone call from this drunk, crying fool last night, talking about how bad he fucked up with JaNair and how he was going to drive to her house to get her back. We went back and forth for about an hour on him staying his drunk ass out before I heard a big thud and this nigga snoring loud as hell. I called his phone this morning, and Manny answered it, telling me about all the damage this nigga did in the kitchen."

Toby shook his head. "I've never seen him like this." He turned around to face me. "There's no way he can go up to the hospital in his condition."

"The hell he won't!" I snapped. "Y'all treating this nigga like he's a hopeless case or something. Fuck all of that! Even if my niece has the smallest possibility of being his, he needs to get his ass up there to take that test. Didn't nobody tell him to cheat on his girlfriend with all these bitches. Now you wanna turn around and be remorseful when she finds out. Where was all this remorse when he was sneaking off with LaLa or digging Mya's back out not too long ago on his desk?"

At that moment, Gerald looked over at me with shocked eyes. I guessed he was tripping off the fact that I knew about Jerome fucking Mya. He looked at Toby with his eyebrows raised, and Toby just shrugged his shoulders.

I didn't know what made me snap on them at the time, but I did. Someone needed to stop making excuses for this grown-ass man, and since his boys weren't, I would.

I walked over to the couch and looked down at this nigga. You could see dried-up spots of vomit all over his face. He lay there, his eyes closed, with his arm across his face, blocking out the light. I just stared at him for a minute.

Pathetic, I thought.

JaNair and I weren't the best of friends, but I knew she was probably the best thing that had ever happened to him, and he had fucked it all up behind a ho and a quick fuck with my sister.

"Jerome!" I slapped his arm away from his face. "Get your bitch ass up and get ready to go on up to this hospital."

He rolled over and groaned.

"I don't wanna hear that shit!" I growled. "Get your ass up, go wash your face, drink you a cup of coffee, and have your ass out to that car in ten minutes. Don't nobody have time for this bullshit. It's because of you and your dick that you have to go take this test."

He still wasn't budging, so I picked up the pitcher of water next to the couch and poured the whole thing over his head. That nigga jumped up so fast, I almost got whiplash.

"After you finish this little business you have with my sister, you're more than welcome to take your ass home and drink yourself to death." And with that said, I turned around and started for the door. Both Toby and Gerald stood there with their mouths open wide, in shock. It was very rare that I got on some hood shit, but sometimes you just couldn't help it. Especially with these nothing-ass niggas.

"Y'all got ten minutes to have fuck boy outside," I said over my shoulder as I left that stanking-ass office.

Jerome

My head was spinning as I stood in the hospital room, waiting to take this DNA test. For the life of me, I couldn't remember anything that had happened after closing last night, other than drinking damn near half of our liquor inventory. Thinking back now with half a sober mind, I did recall singing and leaving messages on JaNair's voicemail one minute, then crying like a baby and cussing her out for not picking up any of my calls the next. Shit was crazy. Every time I closed my eyes, that hurt look JaNair had had on her face before she smacked me would flash before my eyes. I knew I needed to make this up to her somehow and someway.

I ran my hand down my face and blew out a frustrated breath. All of this could've been avoided if I had never fucked with that bitch Mya. Just thinking about her ho ass and the way that she had blurted that shit out had me flexing my jaw, flaring my nose, and balling my fist. I knew that to the people sitting around me, I might look a little crazy with the way my whole demeanor had changed, but at this point, I really didn't give a damn, and either one of them could get it. I had some pent-up frustration I needed to get out, anyway.

"Yo, dude, you okay?" Toby asked, snapping me out of my thoughts.

"What do you think, man? JaNair's not answering my calls, I drank and nearly destroyed half of the liquor we just bought, which will have to be refunded from out of my pocket, I'm hung over, and now I'm here at this hospital, waiting to take a test to see if I fathered a child with my girl's best friend. Would you be okay?"

He laughed. "Rome, man, you can't blame nobody else but yourself with this one. G and I tried to warn you, but you wouldn't listen."

I cut my eyes and stepped away from his white ass. I knew that everything he had just said was right, but a nigga wasn't trying to hear that. Especially when I had paid that bitch Mya to keep her mouth shut. On top of the money I would have to dish out for the liquor, I also needed to find a way to replace the two grand I'd borrowed from the company account to give to her ass.

I walked out of the room at the same time that the tech who was supposed to be administering the DNA test walked in. Knowing that I had a few minutes before it was my turn, because of the bodies before me, I stood in the hallway and pulled my phone out of my pocket and hit JaNair's line again. Just like the two hundred times before, my call went straight to voicemail.

"Shit!" I hissed as I balled my fist and hit the wall.

"Sir, please don't do that again. I'm going to have to ask you to leave if you can't control yourself."

I looked the maxilla gorilla–looking security guard up and down. Today was not the day to test my patience, and his short ass was about to get it. Before I could even say anything to him in return, however, a door swung open and a nurse entered the hallway, followed by Lil Ray and Big Will.

"Okay, sir, you can follow me and these two," the nurse said as she slowed her step but didn't stop.

"To where?" I was confused. "I thought we were taking the test in there." I pointed at the door to the room I'd just spent the past fifteen minutes in with Toby.

She stopped in mid-stride and turned to face me. "Unfortunately, sir, I have to take you down to the other lab for the DNA test. There's fewer people down there, and we'll be done much faster. It won't take but a minute to swab the inside of your mouth."

I nodded my head, signaling that I understood and for her to continue leading the way. The sooner we took this test, the faster I could get out of here and head back over to JaNair's house.

When we got to the small lab, we had to sign in at the front desk, then take a seat in one of the five chairs that lined two of the walls.

Lil Ray sat on one side of the waiting room, while Big Will and I sat on the other. While he was texting away on his phone, Lil Ray kept staring at both of us, shaking his head.

"My nigga, is there a problem?" I asked. "You seem like you got something you want to get off your chest."

Lil Ray shook his head. "Naw. I'm good."

I laughed. "You good, huh? I don't think I would be *good* if my girl had two other niggas waiting to take a DNA test for the baby you thought was yours."

By this time, Big Will had tuned into the conversation, and he started to laugh at what I had just said. He and I weren't good friends, but we'd chopped it up a time or two at different functions our girls had dragged us to.

Lil Ray cracked his neck, then sat back in his chair. He looked at me, then at Big Will, and smirked. "It's funny how y'all laughing at my situation when your girl"—he pointed at Will—"left you for a white dude." He pointed at me. "And your girl is on her way to Texas."

Texas? Who the fuck does JaNair know in Texas? I wondered. I quickly wiped the confused look off my face when I realized that both Ray and Will were looking at me.

"Okay, fellas. Who wants to go first?" said the older white lady behind the counter at the front desk.

Without even answering first, I hopped out of my seat and headed down the hall. I wanted to be the first to go and the first to leave. I needed to find out exactly where JaNair was and who the hell was all the way out in Texas.

JaNair

"Man, I swear I've never eaten so much food in my life," I said as I reclined farther in the leather seat of the tinted-out Navigator.

Neesh glanced over at me. "Girl, that's my spot right there. Me and Daddy Duke come here every Saturday morning for breakfast."

"Daddy Duke? What, is that, like, your sugar daddy or something?"

She giggled and pushed her glasses up on her nose. "Daddy Duke is what I call my father. You don't pay attention well, I see. I told you that at the restaurant."

Maybe she did; maybe she didn't. I had been too focused on stuffing my face with that good food to really pay her my full attention.

"No, I remember you saying your father owned the company. What was his name again?"

"Quincy Crutchfield." The look on her face was one you gave somebody when you were trying to say, "I know you heard of him before."

But the truth was, I never had heard of him, so I just shrugged my shoulders and shook my head.

"Wow, girl. You need to pick up an *XXL* or *Vibe* magazine every once in a while. I've never met anyone who didn't know who my father was."

She went to texting on her phone, and I returned to looking out the window and checking out the Lone Star State's scenery. I couldn't say that I was impressed by any of this country lifestyle, but I guessed if this was where you resided or grew up, you'd love it.

When we'd been in the car for a little over three hours, I just couldn't wait until we got to our destination. My ass was numb from sitting for so damn long.

I looked over at Neesh and couldn't do anything but laugh. Her ass was straight knocked out, with her mouth wide open and drool falling down her chin. The grease spot on the window spread wider and wider every time the truck hit a bump.

After another twenty minutes, we finally exited the freeway somewhere in Houston and turned into a place called the Galleria. From the many storefronts on the outside, I could only assume that we were at some sort of mall.

"Neesh," I called out, but I received no answer, because she was still sound asleep. I nudged her a bit and called her name again, but I couldn't get a reaction. It took me smacking her on the cheek a few times to finally wake her up.

"Why are we at a mall?" I asked her.

She stretched her limbs and yawned before taking in her surroundings. "Oh, I advised Mr. Jones that you arrived without a piece of luggage in sight." She yawned again. "So he told me to stop here to get you whatever personal items you needed and a few outfits for right now. Damn, I was sleeping good as hell. Them grits will do it to you every time."

I sat back in my seat, smiling on the inside and outside. Semaj sure knew how to make a girl feel welcomed. I just might like it out here in Texas, after all.

Damn near three hours later, I was dropped off at the high-rise building Semaj had been living in since he got here and would be residing in for the rest of his stay. I didn't need a key to get in the building, because he had already called the concierge and advised them of my arrival.

When I took the elevator up to his floor and then walked into his three-bedroom, two-and-a-half-bath condo, I was in complete awe. The spacious living quarters could probably be featured in any *Home Living Magazine*. There was a hardwood floor throughout the whole unit. The open-concept kitchen was beyond gorgeous, with its stainless-steel appliances. The ample living room had plenty of space to entertain, even with the modern and very expensive furniture it featured. I walked over to the floor-to-ceiling windows and fell in love with the beautiful, romantic view of downtown Houston. I was so engrossed with the view before me that I didn't even hear the bellhop leave.

While exploring the rest of the condo, I became familiar with just about every square foot of it, from the pantry in the kitchen downstairs to all three bedrooms and bathrooms upstairs. I even found out where the pool was just by stepping out onto the balcony to look at the view again.

I placed the few bags that I had in what I assumed was one of the guest rooms. There were no signs that anyone slept in that room, so it had to be reserved for me. I thought about just going into the master bedroom and making myself comfortable, but I didn't know what I would do if Semaj came home with company. So to save myself from being embarrassed, I decided to relax in the guest room.

After getting settled a bit and taking a shower, I hopped in the soft queen-size bed and waited for Semaj to return home. With the room being so quiet, jet lag kicking in from my flight earlier, and the lack of rest I'd had in the past twenty-four hours, I fell asleep.

When I woke up the next morning, I was refreshed and ready to explore the country city of Houston. I made the bed and tidied up a bit, then went to brush my teeth and wash my face. I didn't know for certain if Semaj was here, but I was pretty sure that he was. Last night my sleep had been momentarily disrupted when I thought I heard someone come into the room for a quick second, then leave right away. Then the smell of weed and Semaj's favorite Tom Ford cologne had hit me smack in the face. I had wanted to get up so bad to see him, but I was so sleepy that I figured I'd see him in the morning.

I swear the butterflies in my stomach started to dance around the minute I stepped out of my room. I headed down the hall to the closed doors of the master suite. I knocked a couple of times but got no answer. When I put my ear to one of the doors, I could hear the faint sound of a shower running. I thought about going in there to join him but decided to let that happen a little later. Instead, I hurried down to the kitchen and looked for something to make us for breakfast.

Since the refrigerator and the cabinets were fully stocked, I didn't have any problem finding something to cook. A meat lover's omelet, toast, hash browns, and a cup of orange juice was on the menu this morning.

It took about thirty minutes to get everything done and our plates made. I'd left my phone upstairs in the guest room, so I set the table, then ran back up there to get it.

It took me about fifteen minutes to locate my phone. The damn thing had died, and I forgot where I'd placed it. After looking on and under the bed, in the closet and the bathroom, I finally found it behind the dresser. How it had got there, I couldn't even tell you.

I was making my way back down to the kitchen when I passed the now open doors to the master suite. Excitement totally filled me, so I put a little pep in my step and flew down the stairs with the biggest smile on my face.

However, that smile instantly became a frown when my eyes landed on the thick, curvy backside of some girl in a flowery silk kimono. Her hair was in a neat ponytail at the back of her head, while her bare feet dangled from the chair she was sitting on. Not only had the bitch drunk both cups of orange juice, but she also had the nerve to be eating the food on one of the plates I had just made.

I silently drew closer to her. When I was a few feet behind her, I said sternly, "Um, excuse me! I don't know who you are or why you are here, but that breakfast isn't for you."

She took a few more bites of the omelet, then put the fork down. She just sat there, while I stood in complete silence. Finally, she decided to turn around.

For a quick second, an insecure feeling ran through my body. This chick was gorgeous. Her slanted light brown eyes almost had me mesmerized. Her high cheekbones, perfectly arched eyebrows, and thick brown lips got tens all across the board. The only thing that didn't look good on her was the medium-size scar she had on her face, a scar that started at the bottom of her chin, went along her jawline, and stopped before her sideburns.

"You must be Semaj's cousin Janet, yes?" She stuck her hand out for me to shake. I looked at it and turned my nose up, then looked back down at her. A silly smirk was on her face.

"Naw, baby girl, I'm not related to Semaj in any type of way," I answered, letting the truth be known. "And my name is JaNair, not Janet, which I'm pretty sure you know."

She shrugged her shoulders. "Maybe I just don't care." This mystery chick didn't have an accent as thick as Neesh's, but I could hear a little Southern twang some-where in there.

"So, who are you? I mean, at least let me know your name. You down here eating the breakfast that I just made and all," I said as I walked over to the kitchen counter. I needed her to really see that I hadn't flown all the way out here just to see that Semaj now had a live-in girlfriend and then to go home. I was staying for my little vacation whether she liked it or not.

"My name is Kwency . . ."

I looked at her neck to see if she had an Adam's apple. I prayed like hell Semaj wasn't swinging that way now. When I didn't see one, I let out the breath that I was holding. This bitch didn't look like a man, but you couldn't tell nowadays, so I had to ask about this unique name.

"Quincy? Like the man's name?"

"Yes, like the man's name." She rolled her eyes. "But it's spelled differently, and just in case you're wondering, no, I am not a man. I'm all woman," she said as she stood, opened her robe, and revealed the red lace bra and panty set she had on. I was so amazed at the structure of her body that I probably would've stared at her for a long time if the front door to the condo hadn't opened at that very moment.

When I turned around, my pussy instantly started to get wet. Semaj walked through that muthafucka, lookin' sexy as hell but tired as fuck.

Immediately, I became self-conscious about standing next to this Kwency chick. She was out here looking like a superthick Victoria's Secret model; and with my tights, wifebeater, and a rainbow scarf wrapped around my head, I was looking like I was at a slumber party.

He threw his keys on the end table and his backpack on the couch. His eyes shifted between ole girl and me as he walked toward us until he was fully in the kitchen. He grabbed me into one of the tightest hugs, damn near lifting me off the floor. We stayed in our embrace for a minute, silently telling each other how much we had missed one another and enjoying each other's scent.

When he finally let me go, he smiled at me, then walked to the kitchen table, taking a bag of weed, some wraps, and a lighter out of his pocket as he went.

"Jay, you already know we got some catching up to do, and we'll get up with that later. Kwency, I don't even wanna know why you in my shit, damn near naked, like you live here. You can get your stuff and go. Make sure you leave my key on the counter before you do. I'm about to smoke this blunt, take a shower, then go to sleep. I'll see you later on, Kwency. And, Jay, I'll see you when I get up." He didn't even turn around and address us. We were looking at his back the whole time he was talking.

I looked at Kwency, who rolled her eyes and left the kitchen. I put the single full plate in the microwave, then cleaned the dirty one. After seeing ole girl out and retrieving that key, I went to my room and charged my phone. I needed to call Neesh and see what the deal was with Semaj and this Kwency chick.

Mya

I knew that for the next couple of weeks or so, I needed to lay low if I wanted to keep my face from being beaten in. The look Jerome and LaLa had had on their faces when I left the club that night had sent a chill down my spine. Revealing that little bit of information to JaNair may work in my favor, though. If I knew my cousin, which I really did, she was not talking to either one of them right now. Probably had even blocked them from calling her phone and everything.

That was what that bitch LaLa got, though. I never did like her ass. I guessed the fact that we were so much alike was one of the main reasons, but there was just something off with her vibe to me. I knew I should be the last one to talk about the next bitch's pussy, but I wasn't surprised one bit that she had fucked Big Will. Quiet as kept, we had fooled around a few times too. Never had had sex, but I'd given him some head on two different occasions. We'd been drunk and kicking it after a night of partying. Niecey had been at work and hadn't been able to get off those two times. Sometimes I wondered whether I would even like it if we went all the way. Niecey was always talking about how big his dick was but how wack he was in bed. Oh well, I was on to bigger and better things, anyway.

I tilted my neck to the side to try to ease the crook out of my neck. I'd been sleeping in my car for the past couple of nights because once again Cassan had locked me out of the house. The first time it happened, I had thought it was a mistake, but now that this was the third time, I highly doubted that it was. Ever since we had had that little STD scare, whatever type of relationship you would say we had had seemed to go further and further down the drain.

I looked at the time on my dashboard. It was a quarter to eight, which meant Cassan would be leaving for work soon. I needed to get up to the apartment before he left, or I'd have to wait until he got off later on tonight.

My phone, which was now on one bar, started to vibrate in my hand. I looked down at the screen. Because the number was private, I sent the call straight to voice-mail. Whoever it was would leave a message if it was important.

I eased out of my car and pulled down my wrinkled skirt, which happened to be the same one I had worn on the night of the party. I didn't have a single piece of clothing in my car to change into, so I had had to stay in these clothes for the past two days.

I looked around the parking lot. Some little kids were playing football, while others stood around, passing a blunt. The little Mexican dude who was always fixing cars was laid up under one, with that circus music blasting. I nodded my head and waved hello to a few of the older people sitting on their stoops as I passed them.

When I finally reached Cassan's complex, I looked up and was happy when I noticed his bathroom window was open. That meant he was still here and I could get in. That nigga never left the house without making sure everything was closed and locked.

When I stepped up to the front door, the strong smell of Pine-Sol assaulted my nose, and a smile spread across my face. A few days ago, this nigga had wanted me to scrub his kitchen floor. I mean, it was the least I could do, seeing as I was staying at his house rent free, but you know a bitch like me wasn't about to do that shit. I had promised that I would and never had. I knew he'd get mad, but eventually, he'd get over it and just do it himself. Now all I had to do when I got inside was break his fine ass off; then we'd be good again.

I knocked on the door, then smoothed out my outfit as best I could and fluffed my tangled hair. I wanted to look a little presentable while looking like hell. It was his fault that I was funky and wrinkled and my hair was out of control. He needed to feel sorry about the way he'd been treating me.

Two minutes passed, and there was still no answer, so I knocked on the door a little harder and even kicked it once or twice. I heard footsteps shuffling toward the front. With a big smile plastered on my face, I lifted my shoulders and waited for him to let me in.

When the door opened, I swear my whole demeanor changed in two seconds flat. I was now in defense mode and ready for whatever was about to happen in this moment.

"Who the fuck are you? And why are you answering my nigga's door?" I muttered.

The bitch smirked and opened the door a little wider. My blood started to boil the minute I saw this ho was wrapped up in one of my new towels, looking like she had just got out of the shower.

"I'm sorry. Are you sure you have the right apartment?" she asked. "Last time I checked, it was my nigga who stayed here."

"*Your* nigga? Bitch, you crazy as hell. How can he be *your* nigga when I've been staying here and fucking him every night for the past few months?" I didn't know what this ho thought, but she had the wrong one today.

"So you must be Mya." She looked me up and down. "San told me you were a pretty girl. I didn't believe him at first, because we have two different definitions of *pretty*. But I must say, he wasn't lying this time."

I scrunched my nose up at this Tika Sumpter–looking bitch. I didn't have a problem with licking some pussy on special occasions for my man, but as an everyday thing, hell naw. Cassan and whoever this chick was really had another thing coming if they thought we were about to be on some *Three's Company* shit.

"Look, I don't know who you are, and at this moment, I really don't care. I just need you to move out of the way so that I can get in my apartment. Stay in your lane before you get fucked up."

She let out this hearty laugh, like I had just said the funniest shit to her. When she finally stopped laughing, she cut her eyes at me and just stared. The smile on her face was now tight, while her nose started to flair out a bit.

If I were any normal bitch, I'd probably be scared, but since I was Mya, her change in attitude didn't scare me one bit.

"The day you fuck me up will be the day the devil himself is sitting on the corner, selling ice cream cones. You know, for you to be such a pretty girl, you sure are slow as fuck. If the nigga you supposedly live with doesn't let you into his house after a few days, what is that telling you? You know he's been here, because I'm sure you saw his car the two times you camped out all night in the parking lot." She turned and pointed toward the living room. "We were sitting there on that comfy couch, enjoying movies and shit, when you came knocking on the door and blowing his phone up." She laughed. "Oh, and to answer your question, I'm Ajarrah Samson, Cassan Samson's wife."

My eyes grew two times their size when she said "wife." There were no signs of a woman living here at all. I'd snooped around and examined damn near everything Cassan owned here, and I'd never found any evidence of a wife.

"Oh shit! He never told you, huh?" she said when I remained silent.

I unknowingly shook my head, still in shock.

"Damn, that's so unlike him. Cassan normally tells his hoes that his wife, who's been in prison for the past three years, is on her way home. That way y'all don't get too attached."

"Y'all?" I asked, confused. I knew I was the last one to get mad at someone cheating on me, but it still never felt good.

"I hope you didn't think that you were the only one. Sweetheart, I've been gone for almost four years. I didn't think for one second that Cassan would be faithful. What man would? We had an agreement. He was able to fuck around, as long as he didn't get anyone pregnant, didn't move anyone in, and kept it real with me. However, I am confused as to why he went against our shacking-up rule and moved you in and not anyone else."

"Because ain't no other bitch fucking with me when it comes to my head game. Plus, my pussy just does something to him. I hope you didn't sit in the wet spot I made the other night."

"Girl, please. The bed was thrown out the first day I got out, just like the rest of your shit. That nigga knows better than to try to fuck me here. This was a place used for his hoes. He isn't crazy enough to take you to the home we share in Palos Verdes Estates. That would've gotten him fucked up."

"Wait a minute! Did you say my stuff was thrown out?"

"Uh . . . yeah . . . a few days ago. You can come in and take a look if you want."

Before she had finished what she was saying, I had already barged into the apartment. All the big furniture was still there, but everything else was gone. The cupboards and the hallway closets were bare. The bedroom where all my plastics crates and bags were . . . totally cleaned out. Even the kitchen was empty and wiped down. I walked back into the living room, stunned. That nigga Cassan was going to hear my mouth and replace all my shit.

"I told you your shit was gone." Her voice broke me from my train of thought. "By this time tomorrow, everything else in here will be gone too. There's no need for this place anymore. Especially when wifey is home," she said as she opened the door and signaled for me to get out.

I wanted to go off on her and slap the smirk off her face, but I couldn't move. I was literally stuck where I was standing. Not only did I not have a piece of clothing to my name, but I also didn't have anywhere else to stay. Niecey wasn't talking to me, Jerome and JaNair wouldn't answer my calls, LaLa was out of the question, and Ryan had changed his number.

Not trying to entertain this bitch anymore, I walked out of the apartment and headed to my car.

I was scrolling through my phone as I walked, trying to find somebody to call, when I heard someone yell, "Excuse me!" The voice was deep and sounded kind of sexy. Normally, I'd turn around and flirt a little bit, but right now, I had other things to do, so I kept walking.

"Aye, excuse me, Mama! I wasn't trying to holla or anything, because I got a girl. But wasn't you the one that pulled up in the silver Camry?"

I finally stopped and turned around when I heard him mention my car. As expected, he was a cutie, in a Lance Gross kind of way.

"Yeah, that was me. Why?"

He had a weird look on his face and shook his head. "Do you have someone you can call to come get you or something?"

It was my turn to have a weird look on my face. "Why? What's wrong with my car? I didn't park it in a tow zone."

"Shit, that might've worked better for you if you had. While me and my boys were out there smoking, they came and repossessed yo' shit, Ma."

"Nigga, stop lying." I laughed. "If you trying to holla, then holla. I don't bite."

He looked me up and down, then licked his lips. "I'm saying, you fine and all, but like I told you a few seconds ago, I got a girl. I'm just looking out for you and shit. I didn't want you to get out there and start going crazy because your shit was gone."

The serious look on his face told me that he wasn't bullshitting. After thanking him for the info, I ran to the lot, and sure enough, the spot where I had parked my car was now empty. A business card lying on the ground caught my attention, so I picked it up and took a closer look.

EDUARDO'S TOWING AND COLLECTION SERVICE was on the front, and the number to my finance company was on the back.

No place to live, and now no car to drive. Could my life really get any worse than this?

Semaj

I swear, as soon as I walked into my house and saw Jay standing in the kitchen, my dick became rock hard. Even as tired as I was, I still couldn't stop my dick from straining against my jeans. The reason why I sat down at the table in the kitchen so quick was that I did not want her to see the type of effect she still had on me. Although I was happy that she was here, I just hated how long it had taken her to come to her senses.

Kwency, on the other hand, that was a whole nother conversation in itself. I didn't know why she kept pushing up on me. I'd told her countless times that I was not interested in her and never would be, but she wouldn't stop. I was starting to see that these Texas chicks didn't like to take no for an answer at all. I'd met Kwency probably four days after I touched down out here. I'd been in the studio, doing what I did, when the door opened and she walked in.

I ain't gon lie, li'l mama was stacked in all the right places and had a beautiful face, so any nigga would try to get at her. Her cashew-colored skin and slanted light brown eyes drew you in. Those forever glossed lips looked as if they could do some nasty things. Her fire-red hair complimented her skin and was always done up. Kwency was bad, hands down. The thing for me was, although her body was tight and her face looked good, she didn't have that wafting scent of peaches I'd grown so fond of.

It was six in the morning, and I was just getting in from doing another long session in the studio. A week had passed since JaNair's arrival, and we hadn't really spent any quality time together. I'd told her that my schedule had been kind of hectic lately and asked her to bear with me. I didn't want her to get too bored and go back to Cali. I was working with this up-and-coming artist out of Texas whom the label had big hopes for. Dude could spit, but he wasn't all the way there yet, so a lot of things were going slower than normal.

Lil Ray had more bars than him, and with that little makeshift studio we had in the garage, he was well aware of what all it took to make a hit and move on to the next. Maybe I should send for my nigga and let him show these country boys what he had to work with. It had always been my intention to put my cousin on as soon as I made it, but I needed to have my foot a little bit more inside that door before I could invite him over.

Looking around my spacious living room, I could see signs of JaNair everywhere. The leftover Chinese take-out containers were spread over the coffee table. The remotes I had so neatly placed in the remote caddy were all over the couches. Her favorite fuzzy pink house shoes, which she couldn't live without, were on top of each other on the floor, and the laptop I let her use was still open, with a picture of me and my baby girl as the wallpaper.

I was tired as hell, but I had promised myself that I would show JaNair around town and do a bit of eating, sightseeing, and shopping with her before I had to go back over to the studio.

My phone vibrated in my pocket, and I took it out and looked at the screen. I shook my head when I saw Kwency's name flash across it. This girl was relentless. She'd been on my head extra hard since JaNair had gotten here, and I didn't even understand why. My boy

Avantae had already given me the heads-up on ole girl one day when I was getting my shit lined up at his spot, Big Tae's Barbershop in the Springdale Shopping Center. I'd never forget the conversation we had.

"So you doing your thing up at Rap-A-Lot, right?" Tae asked me as one of his barbers placed a warm towel over my face.

"Yeah, man. They brought me out here to do a little something for a couple of artists they have coming out soon."

"That's what's up, my nigga. I appreciate you coming in and showing love to your boy. I need to get a picture with you before you leave, though, so that when you start making that Pharrell Williams money, I can say you used to come and get your shit lined up in my shop."

"Used to? Man, if I do make it to that nigga's level, I'ma still come to this place whenever I'm in town."

"Oh, shit! I forgot you were only out here for a few weeks," Tae said as he looked at something on his phone, then frowned. "Aye, let me ask you something, and if I'm overstepping my boundaries . . . still answer that shit."

We shared a laugh.

He went on. "Naw, but for real, I know that the girls in Cali aren't as thick as these corn bread–fed Texas chicks, and with you working in the music industry, I know you've seen a few bad ones. A nigga wanna know if you've gotten a sample of what these Lone Star State women serve up?"

I laughed, then truthfully answered his question. "Naw, not really. I haven't had the time to, anyway. I've been hella busy. Plus, I got a little something back home that I'm trying to build with. A nigga has been getting offers, though, especially from this girl named Kwency, who works at the label—"

He cut me off. "Kwency? Man, I hope it ain't the shawty I think you talking about."

"How does the one you're talking about look?" I asked just as the barber removed the cape from my neck. I turned around to look in the mirror and was satisfied with what he had done. I didn't need to get my dreads retwisted yet, but I did want to get them braided up in a design. My assistant Neesh had told me that she could do it, so I was going to be headed her way after I left here.

"Shawty is bad. Light skin, banging-ass body, with these sexy brown eyes. And that red hair she has is always fly. I think her old man is the owner of Rap-A-Lot. At least that's what she tells everybody who will listen to her."

I nodded my head. "Yeah, that's her, and her father is Quincy 'Que' Crutchfield, so she isn't lying about that. But yeah, she's been throwing it at a brother kind of hard. I'm trying to hold out to see what my lady back home is going to do before I even attempt to look in her direction."

"Nigga, if I were you, I'd keep my eyes on the shawty you have at home and not on Kwency's ho ass. Her ass fine as fuck, but she done been ran through by a few of my homies, including my sorry-ss brother Jayceon. She used to hang with this other ho I hate knowing named Mia Simone." He shook his head. "I swear, Mia's ass could be classified as one of the worst thots ever, and you know how the saying goes about birds of a feather . . ." He trailed off because there was no need to finish. I already knew what he was trying to say, and I took heed. I wasn't really checking for Kwency like that, but if JaNair wasn't ready for what I wanted to have with her, I wanted to have options if I decided to move on.

After tipping ole boy who lined me up, I dapped Tae up, with promises of hanging out sometime soon, and left the shop.

"So is coming home at the crack of dawn something I have to get used to when you make it big?" Although I hadn't heard her walk up, I'd known Jay was somewhere near me before she even spoke. The whole room had switched from smelling like day-old Chinese food to peaches in a matter of seconds.

I turned around to face her and had to bite my bottom lip. She was standing there with nothing on but workout clothes, her ponytail messy and her face free of makeup. I couldn't do anything but appreciate the beautiful gift that the man above had created.

"Sometimes I don't come home at all," I responded, and she raised a perfectly arched eyebrow, with a look that said, "Why not?" etched across her face. "Sometimes I just crash down at the lab. They have a little area before you actually go into the studio that has these big-ass comfy sofas. One even pulls out into a queen-size bed, but there's really no need for that, because the cushioning on the sofas is soft as a feather."

She nodded her head and didn't ask anything else about my nights away from home. We stood there and stared at each other, grinning like two lovestruck teenagers, before she said something about fixing me breakfast. Instead of letting her go into the kitchen to hook up something real fast, I told her to go get changed so we could head out for a few.

"But, J, I know you're tired. I can wait until the weekend for us to hang out. You still want me to go to the party with you, right?"

"Of course I still want you to go. I also wanna hang out with you today. You've been here for a minute now, and we see each other only when I'm either coming or going.

Shit, you've spent more time with my assistant than you have with me, and I'm starting to get jealous."

She laughed, then waved me off, but not before I saw her blush.

"We about to go out for breakfast and go shopping. Then I'ma take you back to the studio with me so that you can see how hard a brother be working and why I come home so late in the morning."

"But, Semaj—"

I interrupted whatever she was about to say. "'But, Semaj' nothing, Jay." I blew out a frustrated breath, because here I was, operating on only five hours of sleep within the past twenty-four hours, trying to stay awake and spend time with her, but she kept on trying to put me to bed. "I already told you, I'll sleep whenever my body just can't take any more of running on Red Bull and Kush. So can you please just go and change so we can get out of here?"

She walked up to me with her left hand slightly behind her back. I bit my bottom lip and cocked my head to the side, which was a habit I had whenever I was on the verge of becoming annoyed. We should've been gone fifteen minutes ago. My nerves were starting to become agitated, so that meant only one thing. I need to go up to my room, dip into my stash, and roll me a fat ass. . . .

"I only wanted to give you these," JaNair said, breaking me from my train of thought and causing me to look down at her now open and exposed left hand. "I figured you would want to smoke on something while I got dressed."

A smirk slowly formed on my face after I licked my lips and took the two rolled blunts out of her hand. I didn't even know that she could roll. I had tried to teach her a few times when we used to have our little smoking sessions back at home, but she had always acted like she couldn't get it.

"So you finally learned how to roll?" I asked as I inspected the first blunt I picked up. After putting it between my lips, I blew a little, just to make sure there weren't any holes or loose ends, and there weren't. The blunt was rolled neat, dry, and tight, just like I liked them.

"I knew how to do it after the first time you showed me. I just wanted an excuse to come to your house for lessons and chill with you," she said as she started to walk toward the staircase, with me behind her, eyeing her plush ass. "Where do you think those two blunts that are on your nightstand whenever you wake up come from when it's time for you to head back out?"

She cupped my face with her open hand. A chill ran through my body as soon as she touched my skin. "I know you've been working hard, doing your thing, and since I'm staying here rent free and all, I wanted to take care of all the little things for you. I'll be ready in ten minutes." And with that, she kissed me on my cheek, then retreated up the stairs to get dressed.

If I wasn't in love with JaNair's ass then, I sure as hell was in love with her now. I just hope she was mentally and emotionally ready to give me all of her, because I wasn't going to accept nothing less.

"So did you enjoy yourself today?" I asked JaNair as we rode through the light city traffic in Houston. After a day of eating, drinking, engaging in great conversation, shopping, and just hanging and having fun, we were finally headed to the studio so that I could get done a few of the tracks I'd been working on for the past few days.

"I always have a great time whenever we hang out, Semaj. You should already know that."

I shrugged my shoulders. "I know a little something."

She tilted her head back and let out a hearty laugh, then playfully hit my shoulder. I swear, I would never get tired of making her smile. While we sat at a red light, I took the opportunity to just take in JaNair and her presence. It amazed me how she seemed to always look beautiful without even trying. Like right now, she wasn't all dolled up or anything. She had on some cutoffs, a white California tank top, and some all-red Vans. Her hair was loosely curled and hanging down, while a red Cal hat sat backward on her head. She had replaced the small silver hoop earrings she had on when we left the house with the diamond-studded hoops I bought her just an hour ago. A little bit of mascara and that red Show N Tell Ka'oir lipstick was all the makeup that she had on. JaNair was the epitome of the perfect woman to me. She just needed to believe that.

A car horn blaring behind us snapped me from my momentary daze and had me easing my foot off the brake and onto the gas pedal.

"Why were you looking at me like that?" JaNair asked as we turned into the studio's parking lot.

I shrugged my shoulders. "I like looking at you."

We sat and stared at each other for a few moments, just lost in each other's eyes and our own thoughts. I wondering if she was ready, and she telling herself that she was ready.

"When you look at me like that, I feel like you're trying to read my mind or somehow look into my soul through my eyes."

I thought about what she had said for a second, then answered her. "It's a little bit of both."

"Really? How is that?"

I turned in my seat to face her and grabbed her hand with mine. What I was about to tell her needed her undivided attention so that we wouldn't have to have this talk later on down the line. I also needed her to hear and understand what I already knew.

"JaNair, I say it's both because I can see that your mind is clouded right now on what you really want. Wait, let me take that back. It's not clouded. You're just going around in circles for some reason, and I don't understand why. You have the flashlight in your hand and a clear view of what path you need and or want to take, yet you're standing at that fork in the road, biting your nails and hoping you make the right decision when you start walking. I never tried to break up what you and that nigga Jerome had, because it wasn't my place to do so. I just played my position as your friend and hoped that one day you'd see the nigga for the fuck boy that he is."

She averted her gaze from me and looked out the window. A few of the niggas that hung around the studio passed by the car but didn't pay us any mind.

"Look, Jay." I licked my lips as she turned her attention back toward me. "If you don't know by now, a nigga is really feeling you, and I want to see where we can take whatever this thing is we have between us. I'm mentally, physically, and emotionally ready to give you my all. I know you just got out of a relationship with ole boy, but that doesn't mean shit. You and I both know that he wasn't the nigga for you, anyway. If he were, he wouldn't have hurt you or abused your time, love, and trust like he did."

She nodded her head but did not say anything. After a few minutes of us just sitting in silence and taking in everything I had just said, we got out of the car and headed toward the building, hand in hand. I didn't know where her mind was at right now, but we had to be somewhat in a good place. Our fingers were laced together, and we were holding on to each other for dear life. I just hoped I wasn't putting too much pressure on her. Before we walked inside the one-story building with tinted-glass windows, JaNair tugged on my hand and pulled me to her.

"J, I just want you to know that I heard everything you said in the car, and believe me when I say, I feel the same way. I just want to tie up all the loose ends at home before we jump into anything. That way, we won't have to worry about nothing or anybody getting in the way of what we are trying to build."

Not truly satisfied with her response but respecting it, I kissed her on the forehead, nodded my head, then turned around and walked into the air-conditioned lobby of Rap-A-Lot Records, still holding her hand. I was all up for giving her that time to handle her business, but that didn't mean we weren't going to start working on our relationship in the meantime. I was hers, and she was mine. Mind, body, and soul.

LaNiece

"You've reached JaNair. Leave a message after the tone and I'll call you back as soon as I can . . ."

"Hey, Jay. It's me again. I just wanted to apologize to you again about what happened. I never meant for things to go as far as they did with Jerome. To keep it honest, I'm kind of glad that it happened. You've always been too good for Jerome's ass and deserve someone so much better. Hopefully, whenever you come back from wherever you are, we can talk. I really want to get our friendship back on track, as well as introduce you to little Aspen. She's so perfect and beautiful. Please call me back, Jay. Okay . . . Bye."

"To send this message now, press one. To listen to your message, press two. To erase and rerecord your message, press three."

Without even thinking twice, I went ahead and pressed the number three and hung up the phone. For the past hour, I'd been going back and forth in my mind about actually leaving a message on JaNair's voicemail. I didn't know what I was so scared of. It wasn't like I hadn't left any before. I guessed her not returning any of my calls or texts was finally getting to me. I knew I had fucked up and all by messing with Jerome and possibly having his baby, but that didn't mean Jay and I couldn't get through this little rough patch in our friendship. I mean, if anything, I did her a favor. Now she could be with the man she really wanted to be with, the man who would give her the world if she only let him.

My baby cooing in her sleep had me getting up from my bed and walking over to her crib. At a month and a half, she was already a heartbreaker. Her curly black hair and smooth almond-colored skin were no doubt inherited from me. Her chubby cheeks, pouty lips, and pointed ears were courtesy of my mother's genes. The three things that threw me off, though, were her big, beautiful, doe-like hazel eyes, her slanted smile, and the heart-shaped birth-mark on her rib cage, none of them a trait from my family tree. I hated to say it, but as the days passed and the nights seemed to fly by, my precious gift from God was starting to look more and more like her daddy . . . Jerome. The results of the paternity test were not in yet—we actually had another week to go—but I didn't need no piece of paper to tell me what I already knew.

I picked up my Sleeping Beauty and laid her head on my chest while smoothing her hair down on the sides. I couldn't help putting my nose in the crook of her neck and inhaling her baby fresh scent. I swear I would never get enough of that smell.

"She's going to be spoiled like a muthafucka if you don't stop picking her up so much," Lil Ray said as he walked into my bedroom with a bag of Chipotle in one hand and a box of diapers in the other. Unlike my baby's daddy, Lil Ray had been a godsend since I brought Aspen into this world. It didn't matter what it was—late-night feedings, bath time, dirty diapers, anything pertaining to her—he'd been right here, like Jerome should've been.

"You know I can't help it. She's just so perfect."

He smiled as he walked over to me and gently took her from my arms. After sitting down in the rocker he had bought me last week, he held Aspen in his arms and began to rock her into a deeper slumber as he just stared into her cute little face.

"Regardless of what that test says, Penny will always be mine."

I laughed. "Penny?"

"Yes, Penny. That's the nickname I'm giving her, and if anyone has a problem with that, tell 'em to come talk to her daddy."

I didn't say anything else. Instead, I took that baby-free opportunity to clean up my room and the little mess I had made in the kitchen earlier. Usually, my mom would clean up her grandbaby's dirty bottles whenever she was here, but for the past week, she'd been on some women's retreat with her church, so the chore fell on me. By the time I returned to the bedroom, Lil Ray had placed Aspen back into her crib and was lying across my bed, taking a little nap himself.

I stood in the doorway, just admiring Mr. RayShaun and the man he was becoming in front of me. When we first started fucking around a couple years ago, we were on the same "fuck buddy" bullshit. Whenever we were in between relationships, we would mess around with each other—nothing too serious, but serious enough to develop some kind of feelings for one another. It was weird, because, on some real shit, Lil Ray was my type hands down. From his personality to his looks, he had it all. For some reason, we had just never gone the relationship route . . . that is, until now.

"What you over there thinking about?" he asked as he shifted on top of my purple comforter to face me, one eye still closed and the other slightly open.

I took in his handsome face. I could tell he'd been to the barbershop in the past couple of days, because his facial line up was still neat and trim, as was his tapered cut. His full, thick lips were a little darker than his peanut-butter skin tone, but they still looked good. The wifebeater he had on showed off the little cuts in his arms and the few tattoos he had across his chest, while the Tommy Hilfiger boxer briefs he loved to wear fit snugly around his slim waist and showcased the bulge between his legs, which I loved to play with.

"I was actually thinking about you and how bad I wanna be sitting on that dick right now." When I went in for my six-week checkup, the doctor had told me that I needed to wait another week to have sex. I needed a little more time to heal from the stitches he took out.

Before Lil Ray could respond to what I said, his phone rang. I knew by the look on his face that it had to be Semaj; it was the only time his eyes lit up and a big-ass Kool-Aid smile was plastered across his face.

"What up, nigga . . . ? Yeah, we good. Moms was just asking about you. She said she was going to kick your ass if you didn't call her this week . . . Yeah . . . Wait, have I seen who . . . ? Naw, I haven't seen her, but she dropped Ta'Jae off probably a week ago for the weekend, said she had something to do . . . Yeah, Mom told me that she's supposed to bring baby girl out there to see you at the end of the month . . . Hell no! You know Moms don't play that. Tasha's ass knows better . . . So how's everything out there? I bet, nigga, you ain't doing shit but staying cooped up with JaNair's ass . . . Nigga, you ain't hittin' shit . . . Aw, man, my little princess is chilling. She knows who her daddy is, so I ain't worried 'bout shit . . . Nope, I'm at her house. She right here." He looked up at me. "La, J said what's up!"

"Hey, Semaj," I said as I went and sat next to Lil Ray on the bed. I wanted to tell him to see if Semaj would put JaNair on the phone for a minute so I could talk to her, but I doubted that would happen. At least I knew she was with Semaj now. I had assumed she went to Florida to visit her parents.

"Did you hear her . . . ? Yeah, man, we just being a little family over here . . . Naw, it'll be here sometime next week . . . I already told you, I'm Aspen's father, so I don't give a fuck what that paper is going to say. In my heart I feel like she's mine. I got first contact with her in the hospital, and we already have a connection . . . Yeah, I hear you . . . Anyways, man, let me go before you have me

waking my baby up, talking all loud and shit . . . All right,
bruh . . . Love you too, man. Later."

As if it was the natural thing to do, Lil Ray wrapped his
arm around my waist and pulled me on top of him. After
adjusting the pillow under his head, he placed both of his
hands on my hips and just stared at me. Because of the
thin tights I had on, I felt it the minute his dick started to
rise underneath me. The sports bra I had on did nothing
to hide my nipples, which seemed to be getting harder
and harder by the second. A light mist of sweat formed
over my whole body. Either I needed to turn on the
ceiling fan or Lil Ray just had me that hot. One hand left
my hip and started to caress my stomach, tracing every
stretch mark I now had and brushing past the little bit of
baby fat that I hadn't gotten rid of yet.

"How you feeling?" he asked in a low voice.

I swear, my eyebrows immediately scrunched up at
his tone. Although his voice was low, I could tell that his
question was coming from a place of concern and not sex.
Even though I knew we couldn't do it, that didn't mean
we couldn't do other things.

"Feeling about what, Ray?"

"About everything? The test, your relationship with
JaNair, us, me."

Wow. Wasn't expecting this type of conversation to
be happening right now, especially with him making his
dick move up under me.

"I mean, how do you think I should be feeling, babe? I
betrayed my best friend by sleeping with her man, so she
may never talk to me again. The father part of my baby's
birth certificate is blank, and I honestly don't know
what's going to happen once we find out who it is. Then
as far as you and I go, we're good, right? I mean, I know
you want to be Aspen's—"

He cut me off. "I *am* Aspen's father."

"I understand that, Ray, but you have to take into con-
sideration that there are two other options. We already

know Jerome is not a deadbeat dad, so if she turns out to be his, he's gonna want to be in her life. Big Will, on the other hand, he doesn't want to have anything come between him getting my sister back. So I'm pretty sure if he is her father, he won't be as active as he should be, because he'll be too mad and blaming her for breaking him and Niecey apart, when that is far from the case."

We sat there and stared at each other for what seemed like forever before he removed me from his lap and sat up on the edge of my bed. There wasn't any tension in the air, but I could still feel some sort of shift happen.

"Wait, where are you going?" I asked when I noticed Lil Ray pulling his basketball shorts up. He headed over to the crib and picked up a smiling Aspen. She was just cracking up as Lil Ray made kissy-face noises and tickled her little tummy with his nose.

"It's time for her bath and night feeding. Does she still have some of that lavender bubble-bath stuff?"

I nodded my head and pointed to the white bottle on the top of the baby dresser.

"Well, open that box of diapers I just bought and get her something to change into after I dry her off," he told me. "Oh, and don't forget to put the hair stuff on the bed too. I'ma wash her hair, so I need the baby brush and the real baby lotion, not that generic shit you use on your ashy ass."

I couldn't do anything but laugh as I got up and retrieved the things he had requested. Man, even if Jerome decided to be a deadbeat and Big Will continued to remain an asshole, my baby wouldn't have shit to worry about in the Daddy department. The only thing she needed now was for her godmommy to be back on board, and then she'd be really straight.

Jerome

"Aye, bruh, I hate to say this, but I think we might have another problem with the waitresses or waiters giving out free drinks or stealing from the register again."

I rubbed my temples to try to soothe the headache that seemed to never want to go away. I didn't know why, but ever since JaNair had left, my head hadn't stopped hurting. Either it was that or all the alcohol I'd been drinking.

"What are you talking about, Toby?" I asked as I went in my desk and grabbed a few Advil from out of the top drawer. I popped the pills in my mouth and swallowed them down with the coffee I had sitting on my desk. Maybe it wasn't the best decision to drink from my coffee mug to chase these pills, seeing as it contained a mixture of the warm decaffeinated drink and Hennessy. It was seven o'clock on a Saturday morning, and I was already suffering from a hangover due to all the drinking I had done the previous night. What better way to start my early day than with a nice cup of spiked joe?

"Man, I'm going over the books, and shit just isn't adding up. First off, there's two grand missing from the business account. How we didn't catch that, I don't know. Then the receipts that are being turned in for alcohol purchase do not match the amount of alcohol that is being drunk up. Shit, we just ordered a case of Hennessy last week. That normally lasts us a minute when we aren't having an event, right? I just saw an order you placed for a delivery tomorrow for our third case in a week. Either

I'm right with my assumption or some weird-ass shit is definitely going on."

I heard everything Toby just got through saying, but I wasn't paying an ounce of attention to his ass. The notification icon on my Google alerts had gone off, so I was all into my computer screen, checking shit out. Ever since I had found out that that snake-headed muthafucka was in Texas, I'd been low key keeping tabs on him via the internet. I had it programmed so that anytime he posted to any of his social media sites, I would get notified.

So far, I hadn't seen any pictures of JaNair posted up with his bitch ass. Just a gang of photos with some famous people and some people I'd never seen before. Always in a studio setting or out to eat somewhere. He had even posted a picture of this badass redheaded broad standing next to a short, thick-ass chick with glasses. If I wasn't trying to do right by my girl and get her back, I most definitely would've hit that redhead up. Browsing through his latest post, I didn't see anything out of the ordinary until I got to the last few pictures. They were also taken inside a studio, only this time, JaNair's ass was in a few of them, just smiling and looking good for the camera.

As I continued to scroll down his timeline, my blood boiled more and more. Not only were there pictures of him and Jay out to dinner alone together, but there were also some where they kissed each other on the cheeks and lips. The one that had me hot the most was a photo of her poolside, just lounging and enjoying the sun. You couldn't see her face, but I could tell her body from anywhere, and that skimpy-ass bikini didn't leave anything to the imagination.

Those perky titties that I loved were sitting just right. Her smooth skin was glistening in the sun, and her wide hips and thick thighs were looking luscious as ever. Even her cute little toes were done like I always liked them, with French tips. This nigga had had the nerve to add to the photo the caption *If you're enjoying the view from this angle, just imagine how it would look if you were seeing it through my eyes.* Then the ugly muthafucka had had the nerve to add a hashtag that read "Look but don't touch."

I almost threw my laptop through the window when I saw that shit. JaNair and that whack-ass music producer wannabe had another thing coming if they thought that I was going to let Jay go that easy.

"Rome, man, what the hell is wrong with you? I know what I just told you is a big deal, but it ain't that big to where you wanna go and kill somebody. We'll figure this shit out."

"Dude, I'm not tripping on what the hell ever you're talking about. I'm tripping on this shit." I turned my screen toward him and pushed the laptop in his direction. He scrolled up and down, examining the pictures I was just looking at, and just shook his head.

"Aye, you gotta give it to her. At least she didn't move on to no sucka-ass nigga."

"What you say?" I asked, coming from around my desk and standing in his face.

He raised his hands in the air. "Come on, Rome. You ain't never had a problem with me saying *nigga* before."

"I wasn't talking about that part. What did you say *before* that?"

He looked at me for a hard minute, then placed the clipboard he had in his hand on my desk. He took a step back, then looked at me for another second before he spoke. "I said at least she didn't move on to no sucka."

"And you just gonna let some shit like that fly out of your mouth?"

"Shit like what, man? The truth? Man, you fucked that relationship up, and I'm sorry to say this, but there is only a minimal chance of you coming back from that. Not only did you fuck her best friend, but you probably got her pregnant too. Lied about having a kid with Tangie, and then you still haven't told her that you fucked Mya not once, but twice. When that shit comes out, ain't no telling what she will do to the both of you."

"First off, I only fucked Mya once. She sucked my dick the second time."

"Will that make a difference to her? Look, man, I've known you for some time now, so based off the previous relationships you had, I can tell that you really had feelings for JaNair, but somewhere along the way, your actions stopped reciprocating the love you claim you have for her."

"I see Niecey got your ass watching *The Real* and *The View* again."

We shared a laugh.

"Naw, man, it ain't nothing like that. And to keep it real, my grams used to tell me that same thing when I was out there knocking shit down and trying to understand why my girlfriend at the time wasn't trying to fuck with me anymore after she found out."

I kind of sobered up a little bit at the mention of his grandma. "Aye, man, I know I didn't say it at the time, but I'm sorry about your grams passing. I was so caught up in my bullshit that I didn't get a chance to check on my boy."

"You good, bro," he said as we gave each other a handshake, then a brotherly hug.

For the next couple of hours, we talked about ways to get more people to have parties at the Lotus Bomb, as well as just come to have a good time. By the time we finished talking business, we had come up with a few moneymaking ideas to continue with the lounge's success, as well as a way to cut down on the alcohol, which had started to disappear.

We were standing outside, ready to lock up and head out for the evening, when I decided to pick my boy's brain one more time.

"So do you really think that there is absolutely no chance of me and JaNair getting back together once she returns from her trip to Texas?"

He sucked in a slow breath and shook his head. His green eyes scanned the parking lot once before he turned his attention back to me. "Man, I really can't call it. Being that I was in your situation before, I can tell you that you don't have a chance in hell. Then again, there are some women who believe in giving second chances as long as you come clean about everything and promise to keep your dick in your pants."

It was now my turn to blow out a breath and wipe my hands down my head. "Man, I hear everything you're saying, but . . ."

"There can be no *buts*, Rome. You say you love her, right?"

I nodded my head.

"If memory serves me right, you were going to ask her to marry you before everything blew up in your face. Am I correct?"

I nodded my head again.

"Then there shouldn't be any more excuses. Tell her how you feel, including all the stuff she doesn't know you've been up to, and let it go from there. If it's meant for you two to be together, then it'll happen. In all honesty, I hope that she takes your ass back. Nigga, you looking bad as hell. I never saw you with an eleven o'clock shadow or in a pair of some dingy jeans and a wrinkled T-shirt. Your ass has really been going through it, huh?"

I couldn't do anything but laugh as Toby's white ass continued to clown me and my outfit for the day. I'd been so out of it, either drunk or sleeping my day away, that I hadn't washed clothes or even picked up my good clothes from the cleaners in a couple of weeks. I hadn't spent time with my son, either. Every time Tangie called to see if I wanted him to spend the weekend, I simply told her no, just so I could drink the days and nights away, thinking about JaNair. But not anymore. A lot of things were about to change in my life if I wanted to get my future wife back and have my family intact. The only thing that could possibly stop that was the secret about me and Mya's bitch ass. If I got rid of her somehow, I wouldn't have to worry about JaNair even finding out about what we did. She wouldn't believe LaLa's hoing ass, and my boys would never dime me out, so that left only one person.

"Jerome!"

I swear, I thanked my lucky stars as soon as I heard that familiar voice call out my name. Toby and I were still in the parking lot, talking shit and not paying attention to our surroundings, when she walked up unnoticed. Her being here at this time was most definitely a sign of what I needed to do, especially when I was just thinking about her. Not even waiting for her to speak again, I turned, raced up to her, wrapped my hands around her neck, and tried to squeeze the living soul out of her ass.

Mya

"Agggh! Let . . . me . . . go!" I managed to say as Jerome squeezed my neck harder and harder. If I didn't know any better, I would have thought he was trying to kill me.

"Jerome!" Toby's deep voice boomed in my ear as he tried to pry his friend's hands from my neck. "Man, let her go! You'll never get Jay back if you're in jail for murder!"

I guessed the thought of not being able to see JaNair ever again was what snapped him from whatever trance he was in, because he finally released his hold on me and stepped back a few feet. His breathing was still fast, causing his chest to expand, then retract at a fast pace. His nostrils were flared out and a little red at the tips. The mug he had on his mouth and the scowl on his face could probably be seen from a mile away. Still, that didn't make me stop wanting him to fuck the shit out of me right now. Jerome knew I liked that rough shit. I was pretty sure if Toby wasn't here, I would've been able to get him to bend me over the hood of his car and fuck the shit out of me.

"What the fuck are you doing here, Mya?" Jerome snarled. "You know damn well that you're not welcome in this establishment no more. Especially after the stunt you pulled the night of JaNair's party. You better be glad I didn't find you that night, because Toby's ass wouldn't have been there to save your ass that time. You possibly made me lose the most important thing in my life."

It was either now or never. I knew that I was about to be lying through my teeth, but this was the only thing I could think of to get some kind of money from somewhere. I was getting tired of living out of my old 1992 Honda Civic. I was so glad I hadn't called the junkyard to come pick it up from my storage after I got the new car. Although it was getting ready to shut down at any minute on me, I was still able to drive around to a few places to sleep and to fast-food restaurants, where I would brush my teeth and wash myself off in the morning.

"Even if I keep my mouth shut, she'll more than likely put two and two together when my baby comes out, looking exactly like you, in about six months."

"You're what?" both he and Toby screamed.

"My baby, and yes, if you're wondering, the baby is yours," I said as I patted my round belly. There really wasn't anything in there, but because I had just finished eating a chicken special from Tams and my stomach was bloated from my period about to start, it looked like I had a small baby bump already. If things were to go according to how I planned, I'd be able to get me a room at a cheap motel for about a week or two, some personal hygiene stuff, and a few dollars to put gas in my gas tank, just in case I had to move around for some reason.

Jerome looked down at my belly, then up at my face again. "Bitch, if you're pregnant, it sure as hell ain't my baby. We only fucked once."

"And didn't the condom pop that one time?"

"It . . ." He shut his mouth and thought about it for a minute.

In all truth, the condom did pop the night we had sex in his office, and if he really thought hard about it, he would remember that we never got to finish, because Toby burst through the door when Jerome was getting ready to bust. To be on the safe side, though, I went and got the morning-after pill the next morning. I wasn't ready to be a mother to anyone's baby, and at the time, I assumed Jerome wasn't ready for fatherhood, either.

"Hell, naw, this cannot be happening to me again," Jerome said as he raised his head up to the sky and wiped both of his hands down his face. "You need to get rid of that shit! JaNair will never take me back if this shit comes out. What are you? About three months?"

I nodded my head.

"Then there's still time for you to get an abortion."

"Are you sure about this, man?" Toby's ass had the nerve to ask. "Kids are a blessing, Rome. Maybe this is a sign for you to just let Jay go and raise your kids."

"Nigga, shut the fuck up with that dumb shit! First of all, I have only one child that I know of, so watch that plural shit. Secondly, if I'm not ready to have a baby with someone who feels the same way, there's only one option for us, which is a trip down to Planned Parenthood in the morning." He got in Toby's face. "And while you're worried about mine, maybe I should call Big Will and tell him the same thing for you, huh? I mean, obviously, you ain't doing too good of a job at telling him to let your bitch go. The nigga steady texting and calling her at all times of the night and shit, even after you asked him to stop."

"On some real shit, if you call Niecey out her name one more time, I might forget that we are boys." They faced off for a few seconds, before Jerome backed away and shook his head.

"Man, whatever. You seem to have all the answers for what I should or need to do. I'm just trying to show you the same kind of love."

Toby didn't say another word as he slowly nodded his head. Then he turned around and headed to his car.

My clit started to thump hard as hell. Damn, not only did his white ass have a little gangsta in him, but he was also fine as hell and Niecey had his ass gone. Whenever your man was willing to fuck his homeboy up for disrespecting you, that was some real love shit for that ass.

As Toby got into his car and sped off, I stood in the middle of the parking lot, hugging myself and trying to muster up some tears from somewhere.

"And what the fuck is wrong with you?" Jerome asked, drawing me from my train of thought.

It was now showtime. I gave myself a small pep talk before I went into the scene. Blowing out a small breath, I closed my eyes and began the waterworks.

Okay. Lights, camera, action!

"Jerome, you don't know how sorry I am about that night. I never meant to blurt out what I did, but I couldn't help it. When I saw you about to propose to JaNair, something just clicked inside me." He started to cut me off, but I raised my hand to stop him.

"No, let me finish," I said. "It was never my intent to break up your happy home with my cousin, but for some strange reason, I thought that we had a connection after that first time we had sex. You may not have felt it, but I did. Even though you would cuss me out and tell me to leave you alone, something kept drawing me to you. Who would've ever thought that that something was the child we created that night? You don't know how hard I've had it in the past two months. On top of finding out that I was pregnant, I got kicked out of my apartment and had my car repoed. I tried to get in touch with JaNair, but she's not answering any of my calls. Niecey is mad at me for what I did to her sister, and I don't really have any friends, so I've been living out of my car for the past month."

"What does that have to do with me, Mya?"

"Nothing really, but I thought that you would have some kind of compassion for me since I'm carrying your child."

"So, what? You expect me to let you come live with me until you can get on your feet or something?"

"Well . . ."

He shook his head. "Not going to happen, and neither is this pregnancy." He walked to his car, unlocked it, and then grabbed something out of the center console. "I don't feel sorry one bit for what you're going through, Mya. You've fucked a lot of people over, so this is probably your karma coming back to you. I'm not one hundred percent sure if this is my baby you're carrying, because my memory is a bit fuzzy right now, but just in case . . ." He handed me a check after scribbling an amount, signing it, and ripping it out of his checkbook.

"Five hundred dollars?" I asked. I wasn't being ungrateful at all. Honestly, I thought I was only going to get $350 at the most. I'd be able to get me a room for three weeks now.

"I don't know how much abortions cost, but I'm sure it shouldn't be any more than that. Mya, I'm going to tell you this, and I mean this shit from the bottom of my heart." He pointed at my stomach. "You better take care of *that* by the end of next week, or we are going to have problems. If I find out that you didn't terminate this pregnancy or that you opened your mouth to JaNair about what we did, I will snap your fucking neck next time."

And with that being said, he hopped in his car and drove off.

I laughed to myself as I watched his taillights disappear into the night. That was a great performance, if I might say so myself. I got way more than I needed, and I wouldn't have to sleep uncomfortably in my small-ass car for a week or two. Jerome didn't have shit to worry about with me opening my mouth, either. I valued my life. Plus, I was trying to get my room back at Jay's house, anyway. If what Jerome and I did ever got out, I would more than likely have to move to Florida and stay with my aunt and uncle for a while.

LaNiece

"You've reached JaNair. Leave a message after the beep and I'll get back to you . . ."

"Hey, Jay. It's me, La, again. I was just calling to see how things are going there in Texas. I know you're probably wondering how I know you're out there. Ray actually told me. I'm glad you finally decided to give Semaj a chance. You can tell he really loves you, and you deserve to be treated like a queen. Anyhoo, I miss you, Jay, and I was wondering if when you come back, we can talk about . . . everything. Okay, I'll let you go now. Call me back. My number is still the same."

"To send this message now, press one. To listen to your message, press two. To erase and rerecord your message, press three . . ."

This was the tenth time I'd recorded the message I was trying to leave for JaNair. I didn't know what was going on, but it just wasn't sounding sincere enough to me.

"Shit! I guess I'll try this one more time," I said aloud as I pressed the numeral three on my phone. I was about to leave another message when the doorbell rang. Forgetting all about the task at hand, I placed my phone on the coffee table and went to answer the door.

"Who is it?" I asked as I walked past a sleeping Aspen in her bassinet. My mother wasn't in town, and I wasn't expecting any company, so I had no clue who was at the door.

"LaLa, it's me. Open up. We need to talk!"

I stood frozen for a minute, trying to process the voice I had just heard. I knew my ears had to be deceiving me, because it couldn't possibly be who I thought it was.

The loud banging on the door brought me back from my vegetative state.

"LaLa, come on with the bullshit. I know you're here, so open the door! You just asked who it is, for crying out loud."

As much as I dreaded the conversation that was about to happen, I reluctantly opened the door.

"Jerome, what do you want?"

"Can I come in or not?" he asked, completely ignoring my question. I stood there and watched as he eyed my body one good time, then shifted his gaze back to my face. I wasn't all the way back to my normal size, but I didn't look half bad with the weight I was still carrying. The black sleeper shorts I had on gave him a nice view of my thick thighs and wide hips, while the white tank top clung to me like a second skin, showing my swollen breasts and the little flab I had left on my tummy.

Fulfilling his request, I opened the door wider, moved to the side, and let him in. The smell of alcohol seeping from his pores and clothes almost made me vomit. After closing the door, I turned around and gave him the same once-over he had just given me.

"You look like shit," was all I could say once my focus returned to his face. His whole appearance was all wrong. He was not the sexy-ass, put-together Jerome I was used to.

He wiped his hand over his face and blew out a frustrated breath. "Man, LaLa, you don't even have to tell me, because I feel like shit. Ever since all that shit went down with Jay, my whole vibe has been off."

I watched as Jerome stopped at the bassinet and looked down at Aspen. His eyes were taking in every inch of her precious little face as she slept. Probably searching for any resemblance to himself. This was the first time he'd seen her since she was born almost two months ago.

"She's beautiful, LaLa."

I walked over to the couch, sat down, and crossed my legs under my butt. "Thank you, Rome. That little lady right there is my life."

His eyes, low and glossy, turned to me. "So is she mine?"

A huge lump formed in my throat. I was taken aback by his question; I just wasn't expecting him to be so blunt. "Honestly, Jerome, I don't know. I haven't received the test results yet."

"How long does that shit take? We did do it the day she was born, right?"

I nodded my head.

"Like, two months ago, right?"

I nodded my head again. "We did, but it does take some time. The nurse told us that when neither one of you muthafuckas wanted to pay the extra two hundred fifty dollars to expedite the process."

He leaned down a little more over the bassinet and softly ran his hand over the top of Aspen's head as he bit his bottom lip. "Can I hold her?"

I looked at Jerome for a second and started to say no, but then I changed my mind when he looked back at me with pleading eyes.

"I know she's asleep and all," he said, "but I just feel the need to have her in my arms right now."

I didn't know what all was going on with Jerome, but against my better judgment, I decided to let him hold her. I got up from the couch and walked back over to where he and our possible child were at. After making him remove the smelly shirt he had on, I laid a clean blanket over his shoulder and gently lifted Aspen out of the bassinet. I cradled her little head and small body for a second before placing her into Jerome's waiting arms. The pink onesie she had on was a little too big for her, so I adjusted the part that was hanging over her diaper. The frilly tutu around the middle almost hid the fact that the onesie was too big, but my mother's eye still caught it.

Jerome and I stood there staring down at my baby's angelic face as thoughts ran through both of our minds.

"Who would've thought a few months of sneaking around would have resulted in something as beautiful as this?" he said, breaking the silence.

I started to respond, but Jerome stopped me.

"I know what you're about to say, LaLa, that she is probably not mine, but there's something inside me at this very moment telling me that she is. It was the same feeling I had when I held Aspen for the first time."

I placed my hand on top of Aspen's head and played with her little curls. "Jerome, I understand what you're saying, believe me I do, but when I went back on my calendar and looked at the time frame, I don't think she could be yours. Around the time I got pregnant, you and JaNair were out of town for a few days. We did have sex the week prior, but not the week I conceived." I shook my head. "The only people I had sex with then were Big Will and Lil Ray."

"That may be the case, but there's still a possibility."

And he was correct, so I didn't argue with him.

He stood in silence for a minute, lightly bouncing a semi-awoken Aspen up and down. Not wanting to interrupt their moment, I went back to the couch and sat down. Watching their interaction made my heart swell. Although how she had got here was wrong, I was happy that my daughter had three men who were willing to step up to the plate and be the best father they could be if she belonged to them.

I was just about to pick up my phone when Jerome said something that caused me to pause.

"I'm going to kill that bitch Mya whenever I catch up with her ho ass. If it wasn't for her, we'd both still have Jay in our lives."

The murderous look in his eyes had me at his side in a flash, removing my baby from his arms. I knew he would never hurt her, but you just never knew. I placed Aspen back into the bassinet, then walked to the kitchen to grab the Cîroc and a few shot glasses. Yeah, I know I was just talking about how Jerome reeked of alcohol, but if we were going to be discussing this crazy bitch Mya, I needed a drink, and so did he.

"Has anyone seen her?" I asked, curious, as I perched on the couch and poured our drinks. I handed him a shot glass and took a sip from my own.

"I saw her ass a few weeks ago, when she was claiming to be pregnant by me."

I spit out my drink. "Pregnant!"

He took a seat on the couch across from me, knocked his shot back, then lowered his head to his chest as he rubbed his temple. "Yeah . . . pregnant."

"Is it yours?" I had to ask. Even though I couldn't stand Mya's ass, I hated that we were kind of cut from the same cloth.

"She said it was, then had the nerve to turn around and threaten to tell Jay about us if I didn't give her the money to get an abortion."

"So what did you do?"

"I gave her the money and told her to handle it. I also told her that if I found out that she did not get an abortion, I'd kill her the moment I saw her, pregnant and all."

I sat there, stunned. If Mya was pregnant, Jerome could most definitely kiss goodbye any chance of getting Jay back. Hell, once she found out they'd had sex, it was gonna be a done deal.

I poured us another drink.

"Have you talked to Jay?" Jerome asked, changing the subject. He downed his second shot, then poured another.

"Naw, my calls keep going to voicemail every time I call. I've left numerous messages and texts, but never no response. What about you?"

He shook his head and swallowed his fourth shot. "Same thing. But I heard she's in Texas with that nappy-headed fucker from next door. You know anything about that?"

I lied and shook my head no. I knew Jay was with Semaj, but I wouldn't tell Jerome that. Semaj was good for Jay, so Texas was where she needed to be.

He side-eyed me for a bit, then took another shot before he spoke again. "I don't regret a lot of things, LaLa, but I do regret ever fucking around on Jay with you and Mya. Don't get me wrong. Those three months we fooled around were cool, and maybe in some other lifetime, if I had met you first, I could see us together. But I hate that I fucked up a good thing behind you and her ho-ass cousin Mya."

I knew most people would've been offended by what Rome had just said, but I wasn't. We had got caught up in a few moments that never should've happened, and we had both lost in the end, so I understood what he was saying.

"Okay, La, I'm about to head out. I still wanna know the paternity of the baby when it comes in, because I still believe she can be mine, all right?" Jerome stumbled a bit as he got up from the couch and headed toward the door.

"Jerome, are you okay to drive? You've been knocking back those shots of Cîroc. Maybe I can call G or Toby to come get you," I said, grabbing my phone.

He waved me off. "Naw, I'm good. I'm hardly drunk. I'll be okay! This has been the norm for me since . . .

since . . . since my girl left me." His eyes became a bit glossy, and a look of pure hurt crossed his face. After a second, though, he blew out a breath, shook his head, then continued to the door. I followed behind him, checking my baby while en route and still deciding if I should call a cab or somebody for him.

"Aye, if you run into Jay before I do, can you tell her that I love her and to please call me? Let her know that I miss her . . . a lot."

I nodded my head. "I got you."

With that said, I watched as Jerome walked out, got into his car, started it up, but just sat there.

"Fuck this. I'm calling Gerald," I said aloud to myself as I looked down at my phone. When I hit the HOME button, I was kind of surprised to see that there was a call already in progress.

"What the hell . . . ? Hello!" I said after I put my phone to my ear, but there was no response. "Hello!" I said again, only to hear the automated system.

"Thank you. Your message has been sent."

I took the phone from my face and looked at the screen. My body literally froze when I saw the call time of 01:21:42 and JaNair's name blink, then disappear.

Whenever she decided to check her messages, JaNair would hear the whole conversation Jerome and I had just had.

"*Fuck!*" I screamed, pissed at myself for forgetting to hang up the phone earlier, when I was trying to leave Jay a message. Not only would she learn about how long Jerome and I had messed around, but she'd also find out that he had fucked Mya's ass too.

I shook my head. Whenever JaNair got back from Texas, shit was most definitely going to hit the fan. I just hoped I got a chance to tell her what I'd done first, instead of a recording.

Mya

It had been a couple weeks since Jerome had given me that money, and I was already running low. After paying for my room, then running through Wal-Mart to get the things that I needed, I had only $150 left. As I was sitting in my car, eating my dollar-menu meal, an idea hit me. . . . If it was so easy to get that money from Jerome, I could. probably do the same thing to someone else. I mean, I was sleeping with a couple of niggas at the same time, so it could work, right?

Really desperate times were calling for really desperate measures, and I wasn't above what I was about to do in order not to have to sleep in my car for another week or eat a double cheeseburger and value fries another day. As I finished eating my food, I drove over to the house of the next person I was going to try to come up on. The duplex he lived in was tucked away in a nice middle-class neighborhood. Every car on the street and in the driveways was new or no older than three years old, including his. I knew this nigga had money. He was just a little stingy with his shit, especially if you weren't giving him any pussy.

After knocking lightly on the six-panel primed-steel door, I stood there for a minute, waiting for someone to answer. I knew his ass was here because his car was parked in the driveway, in front of a white Nissan Altima I knew wasn't his.

For some reason, I became kind of nervous as the seconds passed. I mean, the last time I was over here, things hadn't really gone so well. I'd got kicked out of his house for calling him another man's name, and before I'd left, I'd fucked up his new suede couches something terrible. I laughed a little at the memory. I could only imagine the look on his face when he'd walked out of his bedroom and seen all that flour, old grease, molasses, and broken eggs decorating his couches.

I stood on the porch for another two minutes before knocking on the door again, this time a little harder. The faint sound of voices could be heard on the other side of the door now. I couldn't tell if they were arguing or just having a hushed conversation, but whatever it was, they needed to hurry up and answer the door.

"Mya, what the fuck are you doing here?" Ryan asked when he finally opened the door.

I wanted to answer him, but I was so stuck on the sight before me that I had a momentary lapse in speech. I always knew Ryan's ass was sexy as hell, but for some reason, at this very moment, it seemed as if his sexiness had multiplied by ten. The dark-wash Rock Revival jeans he had on hung loosely around his waist, showing off the deep V cut. His six-pack abs were looking toned and right. My eyes traveled up to the Omega Psi Phi branding on his chest. I licked my lips as I thought about all the nights my tongue had traced the outline of that symbol.

Looking at his face, I could tell that he'd been in his barber's chair in the past couple of days. His sideburns faded perfectly into his neatly trimmed goatee, while his tapered low cut was lined up just right. His blemish-free, mocha-colored skin was glowing and had me wanting to jump on his dick right at that second.

"Hello! Earth to Mya." His tone of voice had a hint of agitation in it. "What the hell are you doing here?" Ryan asked as he snapped his fingers in my face. I bit my bottom lip as I watched the veins in his arms flex every time he moved them up and down.

Snapping out of my trance, I shook my head and answered his question. "I'm here because I have something I need to talk to you about."

"Something like what?" he asked as he turned his head and looked over his shoulder. I tried to stand on my tippy-toes to see what or who he was looking at, but he closed the door a little more, blocking my view.

"Well, I went to the doctor a couple weeks ago and found out that I was going on three months pregnant."

He started to say something, but I held my hand up, stopping him in his tracks.

I went on. "Before you even fix your mouth to say what I know you're about to say, save it. Jerome and I were not fucking around at the time I got pregnant. I was only seeing and having sex with you."

"Mya, I—"

I held my hand up again. "Look, I know as well as you do that we're not ready to be parents no time soon. I already called Planned Parenthood and scheduled an appointment to terminate the pregnancy next Friday. I'm here right now to see if you would give me the money to do so."

His eyebrows were scrunched up now. "First off, if you are pregnant, the baby could never be mine, that is, unless you can get knocked up from swallowing now. Secondly, you know as well as I do that I strapped up every time you and I ever had sex, because I knew how you got down. Then, last but not least, you have some nerve coming to my house, asking for handouts, when you fucked up my sofas not too long ago. Thanks to you, I had to buy all new furniture. You lucky I don't send my girl out here to fuck you up real quick for doing my shit like that."

I looked at this nigga like he was crazy. As much as I liked his cocky attitude, that slick tongue was a whole different story.

"Ryan, I wish you would try to send a bitch out here to whip my ass. You yourself just said you remember how I get down. You were there when I helped JaNair dust the floor with that wolf-looking bitch she got into it with over your dog ass."

"Baby!" I heard someone chick say, but I didn't know where the voice was coming from. Two seconds later my eyes immediately went to the dainty butterscotch arms circling around Ryan's waist. I couldn't see her face, because Ryan's frame towered over hers, but I could hear her voice clear as day. "What's taking so long, babe? Who is at the door?"

Being the messy person that I was, I decided to give her a response, since Ryan just stood there, with a dumb look on his face.

"Who I am shouldn't really matter to you at this point. Especially when the conversation between my child's father and me doesn't concern you."

"Child's father? Ryan, what the hell is she talking about?" asked the girl Ryan had brought with him to JaNair's party when she finally came from behind his godlike frame. She looked me up and down with those light brown irises of hers. I could tell the minute she recognized me, because her face went from confused to stank in ten seconds. "You have a baby on the way by her?" She pointed at me. "Your ex-girlfriend's cousin?"

Again, I responded, because Ryan was still mute. "Technically, you can consider me his ex-girlfriend too. I mean, we did do everything couples do. As a matter of fact, you've probably been sleeping and fucking on top of my dried-up juices as we speak." I knew I was a tad bit out of line, but what the fuck did I have to lose? Hopefully, she'd get mad and go, leaving me with somewhere to stay the night and with the possibility of getting some dick. "Yeah, I doubt ole cheap-ass Ryan here bought a new mattress or flipped that muthafucka over after I moved out. He used to have this pussy dripping so much on that—"

"All right, Mya. That's enough!" Ryan snapped.

A tingly feeling shot through my body, and I was almost turned on by the tone of his voice, but that was short lived, as I noticed the way his eyes softened when he finally addressed the Ciara wannabe.

"Babe, go back in the room and wait for me."

"For real, Ry—" she began, but he cut her off.

"Let me just talk to her for a second, baby, and then I'm all yours, okay?"

She looked at him for a minute, then turned her gaze to me. Of course, I smirked and waved bye, causing her nostrils to flare a little, but I doubted she was going to do anything stupid. To get her attention back on him, Ryan palmed this chick's nonexistent ass and placed small pecks along her jawline. She started cackling and wrapped her arms around his neck from the side.

I almost threw up in my mouth as I stood there and watched these two swap kisses and love taps back and forth as they exchanged what I could only assume was dirty remarks whispered in each other's ear. When that bitch let this exaggerated moan escape her mouth, I had had enough. Crossing my arms over my chest, I cocked my head to the side and loudly cleared my throat. These muthafuckas knew I was standing here.

"You can clear your throat all you want, Marsha," this chick said. "You came to our home, disturbing our day of relaxation. Our world isn't going to stop just because you want it to."

"One, my name isn't Marsha. It's Mya, bitch. And I'm pretty sure you knew that from all the times Ryan screamed it out while he was fucking your no ass–having self. Two, your world does stop because I want it to." I pointed between the three of us. "You both did pause whatever it was y'all were doing to answer the door for me, right?"

I didn't want to check her like that, but some females did not know how to keep their mouths shut when shit didn't have anything to do with them.

"Now, if you'll excuse us, Gizelle, I would like to talk to my future baby daddy," I said as I rubbed my belly.

She smacked her lips and turned to leave, but before she disappeared, she hollered over her shoulder, "And it's Genelle, bitch, not Gizelle."

"Genelle, Gizelle, Gabrielle . . . I don't give a fuck! Just take your ass on, okay!"

"Was that even necessary, Mya?" Ryan asked as he pinned me with a hard stare and stepped out on the porch, then closed his door. "Don't try to come over here disrupting what I got going on because the shit you've done is starting to catch up with you. I told you this would happen." He looked at me from head to toe, then stopped on my outfit. "What? Ole boy must've stopped kicking in for you, huh? I've never seen you looking like this. Your hair ain't been done in a while, and your outfit looks like it came off the clearance rack at Fashion Bug."

I wanted to ask how he even knew about Fashion Bug, but judging by the neon floral-print short set his girl had on, I answered my own question. My hands went to the yellow crop top and jean shorts I had on. They weren't my normal name-brand digs, but I thought I looked good in my discounted outfit. However, since his ass had so much to say about my attire, he needed to kick in a little extra when he gave me those few dollars for this fake abortion.

"Where I got my outfit should be the furthest thing from your mind right now, especially when we got more expensive things growing on the inside of me."

He laughed. "Mya, you need to go on with that bullshit. Like I said, ain't no way in hell you pregnant by me."

"Nigga, you was the only one I was—"

"Come on, now. We both know that isn't the truth. Even if I were the only nigga you was humping on, it still couldn't be mine," he said as he pulled the white V-necked T-shirt he'd been holding in his hand over his head.

Ryan really had another thing coming if he thought I would be leaving here without a few coins in my hand. Although he strapped up the majority of the time, there were those occasions when we had not used a condom, such as when we'd done it in a car in front of the house, on parking lot ramps at work, and in the bathroom at a few restaurants. There was nothing he could say to get out of this.

"I had a vasectomy four years ago." Well, nothing he could say except that.

I stood there, stunned, for a minute, trying to figure out my next move. Sadly, I didn't have one. How could I claim to be pregnant by a nigga who was basically shooting blanks? *Fuck!* I wished I had known this shit before I'd come over here. I felt dumb as hell right now. Flustered, I said the first thing that came to mind.

"Maybe yours was done wrong. I know somebody who still—"

"I doubt it," he said after he licked his lips and shook his head. "Made sure everything was a hundred per-cent before and after the surgery." Ryan stared at me for a minute, in deep thought, before he continued. "Look, Mya, I don't know what's going on with you, but you need to get your life together before you really get into some shit you can't get out of. I don't know what all happened at Jay's party after Genelle and I left, but I did hear bits and pieces from the twins. Maybe you should call Jay up and come clean yourself, talk it out, then see if she'll let you come back."

I gave him that "Nigga, please" look, and he laughed.

"Well, I don't know what to tell you, Mya, 'cause I can't do shit for you. You fucked up whatever chances you had with me when you did what you did the last time you were here. But on the strength that we were cool at one point in time, I will give you some real nigga shit, and I hope you take this to heart." Ryan moved into my space and looked me directly in the eyes. "This slick shit you just tried with me, you might want to think about trying it on the next nigga. Especially if he has a girl who lives at home with him like I do. There's a lot of crazy women out there who don't tolerate disrespect or play when it comes to their man, so you might wanna rethink this little scam you got going on before somebody fucks you up."

With one last look, Ryan nodded his head and went back into his home, leaving me on the porch to think about everything he had just said. Should I call JaNair and tell her everything so we could talk and she would possibly let me move back in? Hell naw! She most definitely wouldn't let me come back if she found that out.

I left Ryan's porch, empty handed, and got back into my little bucket. After pulling my phone out of my purse, I got mad all over again because my battery was really low. Maybe I should go ask Ryan if I could charge my phone for a few minutes, since my car charger wasn't working, for some reason. Naw, I didn't wanna have to smack his little girlfriend if she got smart again. After starting up my little Honda, I headed right back to the McDonald's I had just come from. I would charge my phone there, then try to figure out who else I could pay a visit to.

Semaj

"All right, man. Let's do it one more time, and then we'll be done, all right?"

Killa Cole gave me a thumbs-up, then put the headphones back on his ears and waited for me to start up the track again.

"Semaj, man, on the cool, this record is going to be dope!" Avantae said. "Do you think it'll be ready to go by this weekend? I wanna play it at the party I'm throwing myself at Midtown Live in Austin."

I messed with a few knobs on the board, then turned my attention to Avantae, who was sitting behind me. Ever since I'd met this cat, he'd been showing me nothing but love, and a nigga really did appreciate it.

"If I pull an all-nighter, I can have it done by tomorrow evening, fam. Just let me make a quick call to my girl to let her know we need to cancel our plans for tonight."

"Cancel your plans? Naw, bruh, don't do that. You'll never hear the end of it, believe me," he said as he reclined in his chair. "Don't get your ass kicked behind me."

"Naw, Jay isn't like that. She knows how things go in the studio. She's been up here with me for a few late-night sessions."

"Is this the girl from back home that you were telling me about?"

I nodded my head and couldn't help the smile that formed on my face. Just thinking about JaNair always put me in a good mood.

"Damn, nigga, she got your ass looking all goofy in the face and shit." We shared a laugh. "On some real shit, I can dig that look, though. Reminds me of myself when I think about that someone who's special to me."

"Oh, word?"

He nodded his head. "Word. Our relationship is kind of complicated, though, being that she's my brother's wife and all."

Avantae became quiet for a minute, as if he was deep in thought. "I don't know the dynamics of your relationship and all with Jay, but you gotta remember to keep it interesting. Too many late nights at the studio and canceled dates could make or break up a relationship. Especially with hoes like that." He pointed at Kwency as she and a few of her friends entered the room. "All up in your face and space."

"Hey, Semaj!" Kwency sang as she hopped over to me, causing her titties to damn near pop out of the thin strapless top she had on. She sat on my lap like she always did and wiggled her ass on my crotch. "I hope you don't mind me and my girls stopping by. We were on our way to the club, but I wanted to drop in and say hi."

I heard Avantae laugh. I looked over at him and noticed how he kept shaking his head as he played with his phone, purposely ignoring Kwency and her friends, who were trying to get his attention.

"What's up, Tae? You can't speak?" Kwency said.

"When have I ever spoken to you, Kwency? Hell, even if I tried, it would be kind of hard, seeing as you always got somebody's dick in your mouth."

All you heard were oohs and aahs from some of Avantae's crew as well as from Kwency's friends. Even I had to laugh at that. Kwency looked at me and rolled her eyes, then turned her attention back to Avantae.

"Stop hating, nigga! You just mad I never had your dick anywhere near my shit," she told him.

"And for good reason. That nigga Ty's dick ain't been the same since he hit you. Leaking and shit. Then my dumbass brother goes behind him and gets you pregnant." He shook his head. "That nigga knew he fucked up the minute he dropped his seed in that worn-out womb you have."

I tried not to laugh, but I couldn't help it. He was clowning the fuck out of li'l mama, and by her lack of comebacks, I guessed everything he was saying hit home in some way. Kwency was so embarrassed that her skin started to turn just as red as her hair.

I felt my phone vibrate in my pocket, but I couldn't get to it with Kwency still seated on my lap.

"Aye, Kwen, get up real quick, so I can answer this call."

She turned her attention to me. Her skin was still a few shades brighter than normal, but that didn't stop her from seductively licking her lips and letting the lust in her eyes pour out.

"What if I don't wanna get up? I'm enjoying the feel of your . . . phone on my ass."

On any normal day, that shit would've probably turned me on, because Kwency was fine as fuck. That pretty face, thick body, and fat ass . . . But with me trying to work things out with JaNair and gain her trust, I had to pass. Then after hearing all the shit Avantae had just said about her, I was convinced that even if I were single, I wouldn't touch Kwency's ass with a ten-foot pole.

"Man, you heard what that nigga said. Get your ho ass up before his girl comes up here and beats your ass worse than Ceanna did. Matter of fact, I paid for these sessions, and I don't want you or the ho-a-long gang in here," Avantae said. "This shit is now a private session, so get the fuck out."

"Nigga, you can't tell me where to go in this building. My daddy—" Kwency began, but Tae cut her off.

"Man, fuck your daddy. I know who that nigga is, and I don't give a flying fuck. He already knows how I get down, so he ain't fucking with me. Besides, that nigga owes me money right now, anyway. If he doesn't pay me back soon, this muthafucka might just turn into mine."

The whole room went quiet on that note. The assistant engineer even stopped the track Killa Cole was working on, so now he was listening to what was going on from the booth.

My phone vibrated again, and this time instead of asking Kwency to get up, I damn near pushed her off me. I walked out of the studio, hoping that everything would be back to normal by the time I got back and that Kwency and her crew would be gone.

"Hello!"

"Hey, babe. How's it going?" JaNair asked as she yawned. She'd been staying up late and studying her ass off for the midterms she had coming up soon.

Again, a big smile crossed my face. "Everything is good right now. We did about seven tracks already and are about to finish up on this eighth one."

"Oh yeah. That's what's up." She yawned again. "So are we still on for tonight?"

The smile on my face slowly fell. What I was about to say could go one of two ways. "About that . . . Can we do a rain check? I'm trying to finish up this one track for this nigga Avantae I was telling you about. He wants to play it at the party I want you to roll with me to this weekend."

The line was quiet for a while before JaNair spoke again. Although her tone of voice didn't change, I could still tell that she was low key upset. "Yeah, that's cool, J . . . So . . . do you want breakfast when you get here or after you've taken your nap?"

See, this was one of the reasons why I was really feeling the fuck out of Jay. Not only was she understanding, but she wanted to cater to a nigga too. My baby mama or any other female probably would've been accusing me of fucking the next bitch and asking me a hundred and one questions, but not JaNair. That fuck nigga Jerome had really fucked up by letting this one go. I was glad I was there to pick up the pieces and start to put them slowly back together.

I was just about to respond to her question about my breakfast preference when the door to the studio opened and one of Kwency's friends walked out.

"Them niggas is still in there, clowning my girl," she said, slurring, as she used one hand to hold herself up against the wall. With her other hand, she was tugging at the hem of her short-ass green dress, trying to pull it down. "Where's the bathroom in this bitch? I gotta piss like a muthafucka." Her hair was all over the place, and her makeup was smudged a bit. I wondered what the hell she had been doing to look like that.

Not even wasting my breath on this chick, I pointed down the hall behind her and turned my back, then continued on with my conversation.

"Who was that?" Jay asked after I said hello again.

"That was one of the girls that came up to the studio with Kwency."

"*So* Kwency's there?" The way she asked that question told me that some shit was about to start swirling in her head. I could have lied to her, but I didn't want to start off our relationship with bullshit.

"Yeah, she's here, but she's about to leave. Avantae was just kicking her out when I came to answer your call."

There was complete silence on the phone.

"Hello?"

"I'll see you in a minute." *Click!*

I didn't even have to look at my screen to know she had ended the call. I slid my phone back into my pocket and headed back to the studio. If Jay really wanted to rock with me like I wanted her to, she needed to learn real quick that my word was bond. Like I had told her before, Kwency wasn't a problem for us now and she never would be. Hopefully, when Jay got here, she'd be able to see that. Her ringtone said, "I ain't like them other niggas, and I'm not trying to play no games with ya," and that described me to a T. I had finally got her ass, and I was going to do everything in my power to get her to see the big picture.

JaNair

Semaj really had another thing coming if he thought I'd let another late-night studio session go by with that ratchet-ass Kwency lurking around. It seemed that wherever Semaj was, her ghetto Raggedy Ann ass would magically pop up.

Yeah, I knew I had to work on my trust issues if I wanted things to work out between Semaj and me, but let's just say that after the whole LaLa and Jerome fiasco, my eyes were a bit more open when it came to bitches hanging around my man.

My man . . . Semaj is my man. Hmmm. Never had I imagined it would happen, but I like the sound and feel of it. Anyhoo, I was most definitely on my way up to the studio, but not before I picked up my new partner in crime.

Neesh and I had really become quite close while I'd been here. The fact that she was Semaj's assistant and was always around had played a big part in that, but after really talking to her on a few occasions, I'd learned that Neesh was really cool peoples. Totally different from her ho-ass, sac-chasing sister.

I remembered the conversation we'd had a couple weeks ago, when I had finally told her the real reason why I'd come to Texas empty handed and looking for Semaj.

"Jay, you're my kind of bitch. I bet LaLa's ass didn't see that fist coming before it was too late, huh?"

I shrugged my shoulders. "I think she did, because she knows how I get down. I mean, I'm not a fighter or anything, but don't push me."

She laughed. "Her ass pushed you, all right. Pushed your ass right off a cliff."

I couldn't help but to join in on her laughter. Although the joke wasn't that funny, her laughter was infectious, and I needed this little bit of relief. Neesh laughed so hard at her own joke that tears started to roll down her chubby cheeks. Finally, after pulling herself together, she dabbed at the corners of her eyes, then pushed her glasses up.

"I'm sorry, JaNair. I'm not laughing at you. I'm laughing at the situation. I sorta went through the same thing as you."

I looked at her with a raised eyebrow. This was the second time since I'd been here that she'd opted to let me in on some of her personal business.

"How so?"

"About three years ago, I met this dude named Major. He was a friend of a friend, so I decided to give him a go. Girl, a bitch ended up falling in love with his ass after dating for only about two weeks. I mean, he was totally different from the dudes I was used to dating. We would hold hands while we were in public, and he would kiss on me and everything regardless of who was around. Wined and dined me every night. Shit, even my dad liked him. Clean-cut dude, college graduate working at one of the largest pharmaceutical plants in Texas. Major was everything a girl like me could ask for.

"That was until one evening when I popped up at his house unannounced. He'd been spoiling me so much and treating me so well that I wanted to do something for him. Anyways, I get to his house with nothing on but a trench coat and these six-inch heels I could hardly walk

in. Major had mentioned that he was into role playing, so I was about to put my acting skills to work. I knock on his door for ten minutes without an answer. Now, I knew he was there, because his car was behind the security gate, which, now that I think of it, was kind of odd, since he always parked in the driveway.

"Okay, so I knock again, and there's still no answer. I took off my shoes and decided to go knock on his bedroom window, which is on the side of his house, right? I had just got to the bottom of the steps when the door finally opened. My heart starts beating fast as hell, and I automatically go into sexy stranger mode, cheesing and everything. However, the smile that was on my face slowly faded away when I noticed Major and two bitches in a three-way kiss. They were so into tonguing each other down and feeling each other up that they never noticed me standing there."

"So what did you do?"

She shook her head. "I left."

See, now I was a bit confused at the moment. Didn't Neesh just say that we were in similar situations? Her leaving the scene and not tagging at least one of those bitches didn't sound anything like what I went through with LaLa. As if she was reading my mind, her next response cleared up any kind of confusion I was having.

"Our stories are alike because one of the girls that Major fucked that day happened to be my best friend. The same best friend that hooked us up."

"And who was the other chick?"

She looked me in my eyes with a solemn expression on her face. "My sister Kwency."

That story right there told me all I needed to know about this bitch Kwency. If she didn't have any respect for her own flesh and blood's relationship, the bitch damn sure wouldn't give a fuck about mine. I had peeped that shit out the first time I met her that morning in Semaj's condo, and a few times after that. Like I said, the bitch kept popping up on us.

It was obvious she didn't know her place, and maybe that was where I'd gone wrong with LaLa. I'd let her get a little too comfortable around Jerome, with all the innocent flirting and shit, and look what happened. Not only had they fucked, but a baby had been made in the process. Kwency's ass was already becoming a little too comfortable, and tonight I was about to put a stop to all of that.

I pulled up to the address Neesh had sent me, and texted her that I was outside. Although I'd been out here for only a short while, I was slowly learning my way around. I'd needed to use the GPS for this address, only because Neesh had just moved into the Sovereign at Regent Square Apartments over the weekend, and this was my first time coming to this part of Houston.

I looked around at the apartment complex's beautiful landscaping and was impressed. Neesh must've gotten a raise or something, because this place looked way more expensive than the little duplex she used to live in.

"Hey, gayl. What's up?" she screamed with her Southern drawl as she eased into the passenger seat of Semaj's rental car. "You look like you're ready to fight, with what you have on. What's up?"

I looked down at the dark gray sweats and the black pullover I had on. These were the first things I had grabbed out of the closet after I'd got off of the phone with Semaj. My hair, which I had just washed, was in a wet bun, and my face was gleaming from the new moisturizer I'd just used while preparing for my now canceled date. Neesh probably thought it was caked-on Vaseline, given how shiny it was. I probably would've thought the same thing she did if I had worn some sneakers. The white Birkenstocks I had on my feet, though, should've told her different.

"I'm not about to fight anybody. Well, at least that's not my intention. I just wanna go up to the studio and make my presence known and probably check a bitch or two."

She finally sat back in her seat. "Well, you know I'm down for the cause, fighting or not. You already know I got your back. But just out of curiosity, who are we going to go check?"

I pulled off into traffic, taking my time answering her question. Yeah, Neesh and I were real cool now, but were we cool enough? I wonder how quickly our newfound friendship would change if I happened to tap her sister's ass. It was one thing to be beefing with your own family, but when an outsider had beef too, family members usually forgot their problems and united for the cause.

At times like this, I sorta wished things between LaLa and me were still cool. She wouldn't have a second thought about this mission; she'd just hop in the car, dressed for whatever and ready to go.

I looked over at Neesh, who was still looking at me, waiting for a reply.

"So are you about to tell me who we about to roll up on or nah?"

I thought about it for a few more seconds, then thought, *Fuck it.* If she had a problem with what I was about to say, then she would get it to if she came at me sideways.

"I'm going up here to see about your sister. It's obvious she doesn't know when to fall the fuck back, so I'm about to show her how."

Neesh just nodded her head. No expression on her face, just a cool, blank stare, she turned her head and looked out the window.

We pulled into the studio parking lot, still in our own thoughts. Me thinking about how I was going to approach the situation at hand, and Neesh . . . I really didn't know what was on her mind. However, I needed to know where her head was at, so I asked her.

"Are you feeling some type of way about what's about to go down?"

She bobbed her head for a second to Jeezy's song "Fuck the World" before she finally looked at me. "On the cool, Jay, I'm not feeling any type of way about what you said. Kwency is my sister and everything, but the bitch is trifling as hell. She thinks that because our father is who he is, she can do anything she wants and get away with it. I tell her all the time that she's gonna run into somebody that is gonna beat the brakes off her ass for fucking with their man, but the bitch thinks she invincible or some shit." She shook her head. "All I'ma say is I got your back on whatever goes down. Blood is supposed to be thicker than water, but that's hard to tell when the same blood fucks you over and fucks your man."

And on that note, we got out of the car and headed into the studio. Yeah, I did have on some sandals right now, but I'd kick these muthafuckas off in a minute if this bitch Kwency or any of her ho-ass friends came outta pocket. I had lost one man to a bitch in my circle, and I refused to let it happen again.

Jerome

I didn't know what made me go by LaLa's house and say all that stuff to her about the baby and shit. I really needed to stop drinking, but this JaNair situation and her not answering any of my calls . . . I shook my head.

Then there was this mess going on with Mya's ass. I had to laugh at the audacity of this bitch. Not only did I have a feeling that she was lying about being pregnant in the first place, but the bitch had had the nerve to call me a few days ago, trying to get some more money out of me. Talking about she now needed the money for somewhere to lay her head. Had the nerve to say that because she was almost my baby mama, I should feel some type of remorse for her. That bitch was really fucked up in the head if she thought that. I shook my head again. Man, if I could only go back some months. A whole lot of shit would be different.

"Hey, boss man!" Whitney said as I came behind the bar with my empty duffel bag and started to fill it with different kinds of liquor. "What you filling that big bag with alcohol for?"

See, this was why I should've done this after closing, like I normally did, but I had run out of Patrón a few minutes ago and didn't feel like going to the store on my way to JaNair's house. I had already run through two fifths of the tequila as I sat in my office, trying to do payroll, and I was craving more.

Ignoring Whitney's ass, I zipped up my bag and headed back to my office. Payroll wasn't done, but I didn't care. I'd finish that shit tomorrow, if I remembered. Until then, I needed to go shut down the computers and lock up for the night.

Just as I was about to turn the office light off and leave, there was a knock on my door. I inwardly groaned when Whitney's face appeared in my line of vision. I swear I wanted to slap a harassment suit against her ass, but she'd probably do one in return because of the few feels I copped whenever she bent over in my face, showing that fat ass or them big ole titties. I had told her that we could never take it there, but that didn't stop her from coming on to me.

"You got a minute, boss man?"

"Not really. But judging by the way that you can't take the hint that someone wants to be left the fuck alone . . ." I let my words trail off. I could tell by the expression on her face that she was a little offended, but ask me if I gave a fuck. My head was already starting to spin, and I needed another drink.

"Look, dude, I just wanted to see if you needed me to call a cab for you . . . or if you wanted me to give you a lift somewhere. I get off in a few minutes."

I walked back over to my desk and took a seat in my chair, but not before opening my duffel bag and grabbing whatever bottle of drink was sitting on top. Brown liquor, clear liquor, I didn't care. All I knew was that I needed something to drink if I was going to sit through this shit.

Pouring myself a shot of Lighthouse Gin, I watched how Whitney's eyes took in the state of my office. Shit was everywhere. Papers, empty bottles, clothes, half-eaten food containers, you name it. I'd get so drunk sometimes after hours that I would pass out on the couch. Thank God Toby had been busy with his family drama.

Otherwise, he and G probably would've sat me down for an intervention. I knew I wasn't being a good friend to my boy right now, but he had Niecey to comfort him at night. All I had was a pricey bottle of whatever was behind the bar at Lotus Bomb.

The door to my office opening wider brought me back from my thoughts and had my attention turning back to my unwanted guest. I licked my lips as Whitney's full breasts came into view. She had the first three buttons of her top unfastened, so her cleavage was sitting pretty. The little black shorts she had on left nothing to the imagination when it came to her pussy print. Maybe I should just . . . Naw, I was not even about to go there with her. I was just going to stick to my guns.

Blowing out a frustrated breath, I wiped my hand over my face, downed my shot, and stared back at Whitney.

"So?" she asked, walking farther into my office, tiptoeing over the trash on the floor.

"So, what?"

"Do you want me to give you a ride, or do you want me to call a cab?"

I didn't know why, but at that particular moment, I noticed her new hairstyle. Normally, she wore that long-ass weave shit all the way down to her ass. Now her hair was in a cute, weirdly shaped bob. Her plump lips had some kind of pink gloss on them that complimented her smooth brown skin. I just wanted to . . . *Shit! Focus, Jerome!*

I thought about what she had just asked. There was no way in hell I was going to get into a car with Whitney's sexy ass. I needed to get rid of her ass fast. I took another shot and went into boss mode.

"Don't you think you're overstepping your boundaries right now, Ms. Rochon? Last time I checked, your job description said bartender for Lotus Bomb, not friend of the owner." I knew that was kind of rude, but I needed her to understand what her position was and always would be . . . my employee.

She nodded her head while biting her bottom lip. "You know what? You're exactly right, sir. So let me get back to my job as your bartender. Oh, and I'll remember my boundaries the next time I lie and tell Toby I dropped those five bottles of Johnnie Walker Platinum you took a few nights ago. My paycheck thanks you for that."

I laughed as I took another shot. "Well, it's very welcome. Now, if there isn't anything else we need to talk about, please excuse yourself." She turned around to leave. "And don't forget to clock out on time, love," I said, being funny.

Her plump ass zoomed out of my office and slammed the door hard as fuck. If I hadn't knocked the pictures off the wall already, they sure would have fallen then.

After grabbing my things, I finally left Lotus Bomb, a little past tipsy and with no real destination in mind. I didn't want to go home. Hadn't even been there in a while. If I wasn't passed out on the couch in my office, I was sitting in front of Jay's house, hoping she'd show up so we could talk.

Shit, man. What other choice did I have? She wasn't answering any of my calls, her voicemail box was full, and couldn't nobody tell me when she'd be back in town.

Still dazed, I decided to drive toward Jay's house. As I made my way there, the Bluetooth system in my car interrupted my thoughts with a call from an unknown caller. Hoping and praying that it was JaNair, I answered the call after the third ring.

"Daddy!" My son's small voice came through my speakers.

I sobered up a little bit. "Hey, champ. What's going on?"

He was quiet for a minute. "I miss you, Daddy. When you coming to see me?"

Damn! I swear a nigga's heart just broke again, and I didn't even think it was possible. I heard some rustling noise in the background; then my son said something I couldn't understand. Next thing I knew, Tangie was speaking.

"Hello!"

"Hey, Tang."

"Jerome?" She put the phone down and said something to my son, but I couldn't hear it. "I'm sorry about this. I told him not to call you."

Was she serious? "It's okay."

"Yeah, I know, but I can hear that you're in no position to entertain him right now, let alone keep him for a couple days."

"What the fuck does that mean?" I asked as I skipped JaNair's exit on the freeway and kept going.

Tangie blew out a breath. "You're drunk, Jerome. I can hear it in your voice. Ever since JaNair left your ass, that's all you've been doing. Drinking and wallowing in your own pity. Forgetting about everything and every-body else in your life."

She was right, but I wasn't going to tell her that. "Man, you tripping! No, I haven't."

"Then why haven't you seen your son in almost two months?"

Two months? Hell, naw, it hadn't been that long. I just saw that little nigga. . . . *Wait a minute.* . . . Damn, it had been that long. No wonder baby boy had sounded like that.

"My bad, Tang. My mind—"

She cut me off. "Save it, Jerome. Like I told you before, you can't blame nobody but yourself for what happened. Not JaNair, not LaLa, not Mya, not Semaj. *You,* Jerome.

It was *you* who cheated. *You* who lied. *You* who's been drinking so much that you forgot about your own son." She got quiet for a moment, then continued. "Look, Rome, maybe you should just stay away until you get your shit together. I don't want you coming around, just to start disappointing our son again, when Jay comes back."

Wait! Did Tangie know when JaNair was coming back? I wanted to ask her so bad but didn't want to get cussed out again.

"Aye, I am getting off the freeway right now and am headed to your house. I'll be there in five minutes."

"For what, Jerome?"

"To see my son!" Was she serious?

"Did you not hear anything I just said?"

I did, but I didn't care. My son had called, feeling some type of way, and I needed to fix that. Once everything was back on track with him, then I'd go back to worrying about JaNair. Hopefully, she'd be back by then and ready to see me too.

JaNair

"So you just let that trifling bitch take your nigga?"

"First of all, Neesh, I didn't let a trifling bitch take *anything* from me. Secondly, Jerome really wasn't my nigga to take if LaLa got him to stray like that."

"Do you think she's the only person he's fucked during y'all's relationship?"

That was actually a great question she had asked, and to keep it all the way honest, I doubted it. If Jerome could fuck LaLa and get her pregnant, I was pretty sure there were others. Who? I couldn't even tell you. But for his sake and hers, I hoped it wasn't someone else I knew.

Neesh and I were finally in the right studio, after knocking on three wrong doors and interrupting a few sessions. When we walked in, Kwency's ass was nowhere to be found, but her ho-ass friends were drinking and turning up with a few of the niggas who were hanging around as well.

Semaj was so into what he was doing with all those knobs and buttons that he didn't see me walk in. For a minute, I stood against the wall and just watched him in his element. Half of his dreads, which were now crimson red at the tips, were pulled back into a low ponytail, and the rest were hanging down his back and over his shoulders. The Houston Rockets hat he had picked up a few days ago, when we were out shopping, was turned backward on his head and tilted to the side. His red cracked-leather Maison Margiela sneakers went perfectly with the all-black pants and the shirt he had on. He had never been the flashy type of nigga, and the only piece of jewelry he had on was the big face Rolex with the diamond roman dial. I swear, just standing right here and watching him do his thing, bobbing his head, with that gorgeous smile on his face, had my pussy thumping like crazy. I would give anything right now for him to take me in that booth and bend me over that . . .

"How long have you been here, babe?" I heard Semaj ask, pulling me out of my thoughts. My mind was so gone into nastyville that I didn't even notice when the loud music went off. I bit my bottom lip and looked around the room, eyeing everyone whose attention was now on me. Neesh, who was behind me, nudged me forward and right into Semaj's open arms.

"I've been here for a couple minutes. I didn't say anything, because I didn't want to interrupt the magic going on," I said before standing on my tippy-toes and kissing his chin. "Plus, I was taking my time and enjoying the view," I added, referencing how sexy he looked while he was working.

He licked his lips and smirked. "You gone make me kick everybody out and give you your own private session, if you don't stop."

I blushed, secretly hoping and praying that he would. I was horny as hell and in need of a proper dick down. You would've thought that as many times as Semaj and I had *almost* had sex back home, it would have happened by now, especially with Jerome being the furthest thing from my mind. But that wasn't the case. The only intimacy we'd had while I'd been here was some passionate kissing and holding each other at night.

"Everybody, this is my baby, JaNair. JaNair, this is . . . Shit, I don't even know all these niggas' names," Semaj announced as he held me against his chest and kissed my neck. A few of the hoodrats in the back of the room sucked their teeth, while a few others rolled their eyes. I didn't give a fuck, though, because these heffas could get it just like Kwency would if she got to tripping and being real disrespectful.

"What's up, JaNair? It's finally nice to meet you," said a tall, fine-ass nigga with oval-shaped, whiskey-colored eyes as he extended his hand out to me.

For a second, I was lost in his gaze, until I felt Neesh pinch my side. I wasn't checking for him or anything like that, but the nigga was so damn sexy that it had caught me off guard. Not to mention that intoxicating cologne he had on. Between him and Semaj, my sense of smell was in heaven. I shook his hand and nodded my head. That dark, smooth skin, that long, wavy hair, that perfect smile, and those pretty, full lips probably had all the chicks down here in Texas going crazy.

"Babe, this is Avantae, the nigga I was telling you about," Semaj explained.

"It's finally nice to meet you as well."

"Likewise. What's up with you, Neesh?" Avantae said as he lifted his eyes from me and focused on her. "You know, my cousin still asks about you to this day."

"Fuck Major!" Neesh snapped, causing a few people to giggle. "What he asking about me for?"

Avantae shrugged his shoulders. "Same thing I said. Especially when he still fucking with ole girl you used to roll with."

I turned and looked at Neesh. The look on her face told me that this little bit of info was news to her. I remembered her saying that she had caught her ex fucking with her best friend that one time, but I didn't think they were still messing around.

"Oh yeah? Well, good for them," she said, but I didn't believe her. "I'm about to go to the bathroom real quick. Are you going to be okay in here, Jay?"

"I'ma come with you," I insisted. "I'll be right back, J, okay?"

Semaj nodded his head, pulled me in for a quick kiss, then let me go.

As soon as we walked out the door, I ran right smack into Kwency. You could tell she had just come back from doing only God knows what. Her red hair was a little tangled, her clothes were disheveled, and her lipstick was smeared. I ain't gonna lie, the smoked-purple lip color she wore looked good on her and complimented her skin. However, on the tall, lanky dude standing behind her . . . not so much.

"Hey, sis!" she said, slurring, to Neesh. "What are you doing up here?"

"I could be asking you the same question, but seeing as the nigga behind you has your lipstick all over his face and neck, I can already guess."

Kwency waved her off. "You have always been a pain in my ass. That's why I—" She cut herself off and focused her attention my way, as if she was seeing me for the first time. A stupid little smirk appeared on her face. "Hey, Jay. What are you doing up here? Semaj didn't tell me you were coming."

See, this was exactly what I was just talking about. Bitches always wanted to start some shit, thinking you not about to do anything. But this chick was sho' gone learn today.

I stepped all in her personal space, daring her to lay a finger on me, but just like I thought, she did not. "First of all, my name is JaNair, not Jay, so get it right. Second, why would Semaj need to tell you about my whereabouts? Last time I checked, my comings and goings didn't have to go through you, or anybody else, for that matter, especially my man."

"Your *man*?" she asked, with her face screwed up. "When did that happen?"

"Again, that's none of your concern. However, I'ma give you this ass whipping if you don't start staying in your own lane."

"My, my, my, aren't we a little emotional." She laughed. "I'll try to remember to stay in my lane, but I can't promise you anything. Especially when there are a few streets I'd like to speed through." Looking past me, Kwency licked her lips and eyed Semaj, who was coming our way.

Smack!

I didn't even give her ass a whole second to be shocked. *Smack! Smack!*

I hit that bitch two more times before Semaj yanked me back, and the dude who was behind Kwency grabbed her and held her in his arms.

"What the fuck is going on out here!" Semaj yelled as he ice grilled ole boy. "Did this nigga touch you?"

"Naw, he didn't, but if you wanna know what happened, ask that bitch," I said, still fired up. I tried to get loose from Semaj's firm hold, but I couldn't move a muscle.

Kwency's captor somehow let her slip through his arms, and she came running toward me at full speed. A few of her friends who were now standing in the hallway saw what was going on and tried to come at me too. Before any of them could reach me, Neesh jumped in and tagged one of the hoes, while Semaj pushed the other one back. Kwency, whom I had forgot all about in the chaos, managed to run up on me and hit me in my lip, causing it to split. The adrenaline in my body was working overtime now as I kicked off my sandals, grabbed her hair, and started to pummel her face with blow after blow.

"The next time you wanna talk all reckless, be sure you can back that shit up," I said as I let go of her head and pushed her to the floor, where she lay, dazed and confused.

When she finally got her bearings, she stood up, looking rather wobbly, and fingered her hair away from
her face and to the back of her head. A chorus of oohs
and aahs from bystanders could be heard the moment
her bruised face was in sight. Totally embarrassed, she
fixed her clothes and tried to stand up straight but failed
horribly.

"Really, Semaj? You gone let her put her hands on me
like that? After all the shit I've done for you?" she seethed.

"Kwency, what the fuck are you talking about? You ain't
done shit for me. If I were you, I'd leave before I let my
girl get in your ass again."

"And you." She was now looking at Neesh. "You just
gonna let her do me like that . . . your own sister?"

"Kwency, please stop. *Sister*? Really? Where was all
that sisterly love and concern when you were fucking
Major?"

"You know what? Fuck all of y'all!" Kwency yelled.
"Semaj, I'ma make sure my daddy hears about this. You'll
never make another record in Texas again!"

"Whatever! Now get out! Matter of fact, everybody get
out." Semaj turned around to talk to Avantae, who was
texting on his phone. "Aye, man, we gone have to cut this
session short. I think I have enough to where I can have
the record done for you by Friday, all right?"

They dapped each other up. "Yo, we good, man. Just
hit me up whenever you get that thang done," Avantae
responded. Then he turned to me. "The next time you
feel like you might be fighting, let me know ahead of time,
so I can put my money on you, okay?"

I tried to smile, but my split lip had started stinging.

"Let me see your face," Semaj said. He put two fingers
under my chin and lifted my head up so that he could
scan my face. He bit down on his bottom lip as he con-
ducted his examination.

I couldn't help but notice the small smile that registered on his face when he was done inspecting mine.
"Seeing you beat her ass was sexy as fuck, but don't let
that shit happen again," he told me. "Like I told you
before, you don't have anything to worry about when it
comes to me and my feelings for you. I've waited this long
for your heart, and I'm not gonna let anyone ruin what
we have." He gently kissed my only injury, then grabbed
my hand and led me back down the hall.

As soon as the last person left the studio, Semaj locked
the door, then walked back to his chair, which was
sitting in front of the board, sat down, and positioned
me between his legs. I thought he was going to have me
straddle his lap once he got situated, but when he pushed
me back and had my ass sitting against all the knobs, I
knew he had other plans.

He looked into my eyes and just stroked my chin with
one hand, while his other hand fumbled with something
behind me. When he finally reached what he was looking
for, he gripped the bottom of my pullover and pulled it
over my head. He then continued to remove every other
article of clothing I had on until I was in only my bra and
panties. A few seconds later, a song I hadn't heard in a
long time started to beat through the speakers. A slow
smile spread across my face as soon as Jamie Foxx's and
Plies's voices wafted through the air and I realized what
Semaj was asking for through the lyrics.

Please excuse my hands
They just wanna touch
They just wanna feel
They don't mean no harm
Baby, just excuse my hands
Baby, please excuse my hands
I apologize, they have a one-track mind

To squeeze on your behind
Baby, just excuse my hands
Please excuse my hands

With my hands, I can make you do a lot of things
Have you engagin' in some activities you can't explain
Leave my fingerprints on every inch yo' damn frame
With this one finger, I could make you get off the chain
Get to lickin' and my hands, they get they own brain
They wanna touch ya, they wanna rub ya, they
wanna feel your frame

I rolled my head back when Semaj's hands and lips started to caress every inch of my body. With each kiss and touch, it seemed as if he was silently begging me for permission to have his way with me, wanting me to understand that he didn't want to do anything to me that I didn't want to have done.

Instead of stretching out this moment by speaking, I answered his plea by simply opening my legs wider and gripping his dreads and pulling him closer to me. That move was all the invitation he needed to continue his assault on a soft spot on my neck.

A light moan escaped my lips when his knuckles brushed against the soft material of my panties, grazing the tip of my clit.

"Semaj!" breathlessly slipped from my mouth. If I had known a little fight would get me some dick, I would've beaten Kwency's disrespectful ass a few weeks earlier.

Our thought process must've been of one accord, because before I could say anything to him, his mouth kissed my ear, and then he whispered in it. "Jay, I'm gonna skip the foreplay this time around. I already know how good you taste. Right now, I wanna know how good you feel. Is that all right? Can I feel you, Jay?"

Shit. He didn't have to ask me twice. I needed to feel him too. Whether it was his lips on my pussy or his dick being planted deep inside me, I really didn't care.

I nodded my head while my face was buried in the crook of his neck, and I knew he got my answer, because in one swift move, my panties were ripped off me, and his dick was at my opening, getting lightly coated with my juices.

My breath hitched in my throat and I was pretty sure my heart almost stopped when he slid inside me.

"Are you okay, JaNair?"

I heard the question, and I saw his lips move, but I couldn't do anything but stare into his face. His brown eyes seemed to bore into my soul, while his smooth chocolate skin glistened from the light mist released from his pores.

"Jay, do you want me to stop?"

The thought of him withdrawing from inside me snapped me out of my momentary trance. I shook my head no.

"Look at me, Jay."

It took me a second, but I finally looked into his eyes.

"Do you trust me?" he asked earnestly.

I thought about it and then slowly nodded my head.

"You know I will never do anything to hurt you, right?"

I nodded my head again. Deep down in my heart, I knew that Semaj would never purposely try to hurt me, but you never knew.

"If you believe that I won't, then stop holding back on me, Jay. I want you, and I want to feel all of you. Not half or just some, either, but all."

I lay there, taking in everything he was saying. I felt him shift his weight to his arms, then start to pull out. Instantly, I squeezed my legs shut, trying to hold him in place.

"If you're not ready, I'm not going to pressure you," he told me.

"You're not. You're not pressuring me, Semaj." I grabbed a handful of his dreads and pulled him back down toward my face. I closed my eyes, then kissed his lips. "I'm ready to give you all of me," I said, then bit his bottom lip and sucked it back into my mouth.

I wrapped my legs around his waist as he laid me farther back on the board. Buttons were indenting my skin, and the shit kind of hurt, but I didn't give a fuck. My main focus was Semaj and our private session. The heat from his body was consuming me inside, but his face was surprisingly tender. He stroked my cheek in time with the slow thrust he was giving me.

Struggling against myself, I felt my first climax building to the surface only after a few deep strokes. I dug my manicured nails into his back as small beads of his sweat started to drip onto my face. I didn't know if the air-conditioning had been turned off, but it was hot as hell in this studio, but I couldn't give two fucks.

As Semaj started to ram harder and harder into me, the cries I tried to keep at a low volume started to become louder and louder.

"Ohhh . . . my . . . Gawd, Semaj. Oh, my Gawd. Fuck! You feel so fucking good!"

His face was in the crook of my neck, but I could feel his breath hot on my collar. "You feel so fucking good too, baby. So tight . . . uh . . . and wet . . . Fuck, Jay . . . Tell me you belong to me. Tell me your mind, heart, body, and pussy now belong to me."

"Yes, Semaj, Yes, it all belongs to you, baby!" I screamed as I grabbed his dreads and felt my body start to shake uncontrollably. After a few more strokes, and after promising me he would never do anything to mistreat my heart, Semaj cried out my name as he released every last drop of cum he had into me.

He plopped back down in his chair after his dick stopped twitching in my insides, and then he pulled my limp body onto his lap and wrapped his arms around my waist.

"Are you okay?" I heard him ask. But I never responded. My eyes were closed, and I was seeing what looked like colorful fireworks exploding in the darkness behind my eyelids. I tried to sit up after a few minutes to look him in the face, but my body felt as if it was in space and was floating around, with no signs of gravity anywhere.

"Jay, are you all right? Do you need me to get you some water or something?"

"A cigarette would be nice."

Semaj laughed and reached down to his pants, which were still around his ankles, and took something from his pocket. "I don't have any Ports, but I do have a few blunts ready, thanks to you."

Without another word, he put the goodness in his mouth and lit it up. I felt his chest rise as he inhaled the smoke and held it for a minute. He took another pull, then put his lips on mine and blew the smoke into my mouth. Me being the seasoned pro that I was now, I took that hit from him, then grabbed the blunt and took a few pulls for myself before returning a shotgun to him.

"You ready for round two?" he asked as he dropped the roach into the ashtray on the floor.

"Semaj, I'm sore . . . ," was all I could get out before he lifted me up off his lap, then slammed me down on his dick.

"*Fuck*, baby."

"Now that this pussy belongs to me, don't ever deny me what's mine."

I didn't say anything else as I rode his dick until his ass couldn't take it anymore and tapped out.

ShaNiece

Everything in my body right now was telling me to turn around, but for some reason, my feet wouldn't move. I stood outside the apartment that Will shared with his half brother, Ruben, and kept wondering why I was even here.

I was so nervous and lost in my own thoughts that I jumped when my cell phone started to vibrate in my hand. I looked down at the screen and decided not to answer the call, but I quickly changed my mind. This was the third time Toby had called me in the past thirty minutes. For what, I didn't know. Then again, maybe this was the sign I'd been praying for since I got here, a sign telling me that I should leave.

"Hey, babe," I answered as the feeling in my feet started to come back.

"Niece, I've called you, like, two other times. What the fuck are you doing where you can't answer the phone? It's one thirty. You should be on your lunch break right now, right?"

My mind went blank for a minute, but I had to come up with something to say quickly. I didn't want to lie, but I had to. Toby most definitely would not understand me taking the rest of the day off from work so that I could go to Will's house to have this conversation he'd been begging me to have since I found out he had messed around with my twin.

"I, uh . . . I . . . didn't hear my phone. I'm in the dressing room, trying to find something to wear to the baby shower barbecue LaLa and Ray are having in a couple weeks."

"Oh yeah?" he asked. But the way he said it sounded kinda weird.

"Yeah. Remember I told you about it not too long ago? You said you were coming with me, right?"

There was a brief pause before he responded, which was also kind of weird. Something was wrong with my baby, and I needed to find out. I could tell by the way this conversation was going that something was off. Toby's never questioned me about my whereabouts or raised his voice, so something most definitely was up.

"Baby, are you okay? What's going on?"

He blew out a long, frustrated breath. "I've been summoned to my parents' house tonight for a family dinner."

"Okay! So that's a problem?"

"It is when they want me to meet my long-lost twin brother."

Wait a minute. Now I was confused.

"Um, Toby, what do you mean, long lost? When I met you, you told me that you were a twin, so why are you talking as if you've never met him?"

"Because I haven't." He sighed. "I didn't even know I had a twin until about a year ago, after my grandmother died. When I went to the reading of her will, that's when I learned about him. My mother and father had no other choice but to explain who Thaddeus Warren Wright, also known as Cairo Broussard, was to my sister and me when the lawyer mentioned him and what he inherited from our grandmother."

Wow. This was news to me. I thought Toby and I had talked about everything, but I guessed not. I mean, he had told me that he and his family weren't close, so I had assumed that included his twin brother. The only person in his family I had ever heard him talk to was his sister, but that only every now and then.

"Damn, babe. That sucks. I can't say that I know how you feel, because I grew up with my sister. Even though we're kind of beefing right now, I can't imagine growing up thinking that I'm the only person that looks like myself on this earth, only to find out some odd years later that I have a duplicate walking around. So you haven't seen him at all before? This will be your first time laying eyes on your twin?"

"Yes."

"Damn. So that's why you don't really hang around your family?"

"Yes and no. Look, just come to my place after you leave the store so we can talk some more. You have your key, right?"

I smiled at the mention of me having a key to his place. As of last night, I was now free to come into my man's home whenever I felt like it. Unannounced or otherwise. We hadn't officially moved in together yet, but we were damn near there. The majority of my things were there, anyway, and his home was where I mainly laid my head to rest. My mama's house was getting real crowded with my niece being there now, so it was time for me to leave, anyway. Between LaLa, my mom, and myself, that little girl had more stuff than the good Lord could allow, so me leaving would provide the extra room that they needed to accommodate all her stuff.

"Niece, while you're still at the store, make sure to get two new outfits. One for the shower and one to wear tonight, when you go with me to this dinner."

"Wait, you want me to come with you to meet your family . . . and your brother?"

He laughed. "Why wouldn't I? You're my girl, right?"

"Yes."

"We've been together long enough now where I think it's the right time to do so."

"But what if they don't like me, Toby? I mean, do they even know about me? Shit, do they even know I'm black?"

He laughed again. "Baby, you aren't the first black girl I've brought around them, but I'm hoping, with the way that things are going, that you will be the last."

I blushed and became speechless. I always did that when he said stuff like that to me.

"You love me, ShaNiece?"

Without hesitation, I told him yes, and I could hear the smile in his voice when he spoke again.

"I'll see you when you get here, okay, baby?"

"All right."

"I love you."

"I love you too. Bye."

I swear, at that moment butterflies started to flutter wildly in my stomach, and I couldn't help the big Kool-Aid smile I had on my face. I held the phone to my heart, as if Toby could hear how fast it was beating and how happy he had me feel on the inside. I was literally floating on cloud nine and was ready to go home to my man to have this little talk and show him how much I really loved him. However, the little love high I was on came crashing down as soon as I turned around and saw who was now standing behind me.

"So you love that white boy, ShaNiece?" Will asked me, with the meanest scowl on his face. I'd forgotten just that fast that I was standing on his doorstep, waiting for him. "You're really going to give what we have up for a muthafucka who will never love you the way I do?"

I tried to speak, but the words were caught in my throat.

We stood on his porch, staring at each other for a few minutes, before he reached behind me and used his key to unlock his door.

"You coming in?"

Going against what my mind was telling me, I turned around and followed him into the place I'd spent many nights. Everything was just as I remembered, from the large smoke-gray sectional against the wall to the entertainment center, which had every game console ever made. The six-foot wall aquarium illuminated the living room, giving me enough light to see some of the pictures hanging on the wall. Framed newspaper articles from Will's football career lined the wall, as well as pictures of his family. What grabbed my attention, though, were the photos he and I took about a year ago at the little picture place in the mall.

"Why do you still have these old things up? Your little girlfriends don't trip on you still having pictures of me around your house?"

He stopped whatever he was doing in the kitchen and came into the living room. "The key words in your sentence are *your house*. And they already know what it is."

"What does that mean?"

He walked closer to where I was standing and stepped into my personal space. Towering over me with his six-foot-three-inch frame, I had to crane my neck up to see his face. The look in his copper-colored eyes was so intense that a chill shot through my body, but not like the one I got when a pair of ocean-green irises adoringly gazed at me.

"Will . . . I shouldn't—"

The back of his hand lightly brushed against my cheek, causing my words to come to a halt. Cupping my face with both hands now, he kissed both of my eyelids and nose, then pressed his forehead to mine.

"ShaNiece, you know as well as I do that we belong together, and it's been that way since we were in high school. You are my heart, and I will never let you go. Do you know how bad it hurt me to see you with that bitch-ass white boy? Holding you and shit." He pointed to my heart. "This is supposed to belong only to me, and you just give it away that easy?"

I must admit, everything he had just said was doing something to me on the inside, but unlike the hundred times before, I wasn't going to fall for the bullshit any-more. Will was a creature of habit, so it was only going to be a matter of time before he started to fall accidentally into the next bitch's pussy again. Him being faithful was just as fraudulent as bootleg DVDs.

I placed my hands on his chest to back him up a bit. "Look, Will, I'm sorry for what's happened between us. Do I miss you? Yes. Do I still love you? I always will. Do you deserve my love?" I looked into his eyes. "No. For ten years, I've put up with you lying, cheating, and making me feel like shit. For the longest, I felt like your love was the only love good enough for me, because it was all I knew." I shook my head. "But that all changed when I met Toby. Not only has he shown me what it's like to be treated like a queen, but he's also done way more for me mentally in these past few months than you have in the past decade we've been together."

He snorted. I could tell by the look on his face that I had hurt his feelings, but I was only telling the truth.

"You crazy as fuck if you believe that shit, Niecey. What could this white boy do for you besides fuck you for a year or two, then leave and marry someone of his own race?"

Smack! I slapped the shit out of him. My eyes went as wide as saucers after realizing what I had just done. The shocked look on Will's face would have been funny if the situation wasn't so serious.

"How dare you say some shit like that? If Toby doesn't marry me, it won't have anything to do with me being black. It's not like that at all."

"It's not? What makes you so different from the other black girls he's probably dated? I'm pretty sure you're not the first one."

That was a good question. One I'd asked Toby a few times, but I'd never got a real answer.

"Have you met his parents?"

I shook my head.

"Met any of his family?"

I shook my head again.

"Damn, have you even met any of his friends?"

I had if you counted Jerome and Gerald, but that was none of his business. Yet I found myself trying to come up with an explanation. "I'm meeting his family tonight."

Will stepped back from me, and I couldn't help but to admire his handsome face. Ever since we were young, he'd always been fine as hell, which was one of our biggest problems. When you looked as good as he did and played sports, there was no doubt that he'd have pussy being thrown at him from every which way. The same smooth cinnamon-colored skin, copper-colored eyes, full, thick lips, hypnotizing smile, and athletic, toned body that got my attention had grabbed all those other hoes' attention too.

I felt my phone vibrating in my purse and knew it had to be Toby. The last time we talked, I was supposed to be on my way home, which was almost an hour ago. Tired of the conversation between Will and me, I decided to take my ass home. Being here in the first place was a mistake, especially when I knew I'd never again give our relationship another chance.

I started walking toward the door, but then I stopped and faced Will. "Look, Will, like I said before, I love you, and you will always hold a special place in my heart. But I've moved on to someone who I feel was meant for me."

Will opened his mouth to say something, but I raised my hand to prevent him from speaking.

"Regardless of how long Toby and I have been together, I still feel in my mind, in my heart, and in my soul that he's the one. Coming over here was a mistake, and I'm not ashamed to admit that. Believe me when I say that my intent wasn't to give you any false hope about us but to let you know that this . . ." I pointed between us. "This will never happen again. Thank you for loving me in your way for all those years."

When Will just stood there, with nothing else to say, I nodded my head and turned to leave. I hoped everything I had just said to him did not go in one ear and out the other. It was way past time for us to let this relationship go. The real feelings we once had for each other had left a long time ago, and I hoped Will could learn to move on just like I did.

After taking one last look at the pictures of us on the wall, I finally made my way to the door. Before I was able to reach for the doorknob, Will's strong hand grabbed my shoulder and spun me around. With one arm pulling me into his chest and the other gripping my chin, he brought his face down to my level and pressed his lips against mine. I let him kiss me for the last time before I slowly pulled away.

"Goodbye, Will." With my back still toward the door, I fumbled for the knob until I found it and twisted it. I was still staring at Will when I felt myself run into somebody.

After breaking away from the drawn-out goodbye with our eyes, I turned around and came face-to-face with the last person I expected to see.

"LaLa?"

LaNiece

"LaNiece, you have some mail on the table," my mom said as she walked into my room. "I'm about to go down here to the party supply store and get some more things for the baby shower. Are you sure you don't want the pink balloon arch? I think my grandbaby will love it."

"Mom, your grandbaby isn't going to even know what a balloon arch is, let alone like it."

I swear, she spoiled Aspen way more than she ever had Niecey and me. Although I appreciated all of it, it was starting to get a little out of hand. For instance, the cute little Winnie the Pooh diaper carrier I had bought from Wal-Mart had been thrown out and replaced with a Louis Vuitton Monogram Mini Lin diaper bag. The ten-dollar plastic bathtub I got from Ross had been used only once before she replaced that with the twenty-seven-hundred-dollar MagicBath Baby Hot Tub. As if that wasn't enough, I hadn't even got a chance to use the cute little Minnie Mouse car seat I had on layaway. The day I was released from the hospital, my mom already had some shit called the Carkoon strapped up and ready to go in the backseat of her car.

"My grandbaby only rolls in the best," was all she'd said when I asked her what the fuck that cocoon-looking contraption was.

I'm not complaining, though, because I came up a little bit too. The 2002 Toyota Camry I was driving was upgraded to a 2016, courtesy of my mother, and my car insurance was paid up for the next two years. She had also paid off any debt I had that reflected negatively on my credit report. All I had to focus on now was getting a better job and making sure I was able to take care of my baby in the future.

"Let's see what Aspen has to say about this," my mother said as she literally snatched my baby out of my arms, bringing me back from my thoughts. As soon as my mother's face came into Aspen's line of vision, she started making those cute little baby noises and smiling her ass off. "Does Nan's baby want a pink balloon arch for her party? You do! Okay, baby love. Nana will get you that arch."

I playfully rolled my eyes, then took those couple of baby-free minutes to text Lil Ray.

Me: Hey, babe! You still coming over after work?

He immediately responded.

BD: Yeah.

I smiled.

BD: We need to talk.

Then I frowned. Whenever Lil Ray came at me with that line, some bullshit was more than likely soon to follow.

The last time "we needed to talk," I had found out that Lil Ray was messing with some little pop tart named Diamond, one of Semaj's baby mama's friends. She was some hoodrat-ass bitch who danced up at King Henry's, which means she was sucking and fucking on damn near everything walking. What he saw in her, I would never know. The bitch looked like Tricks from *The Players Club*, just a little younger, with those ugly-ass witch nails and a blond weave that touched the tip of her ass. Her walk and her attitude were stank, but she had that nigga's nose open for a minute. So much so that I went from getting the dick whenever I wanted it to every blue moon. Yeah, he and I weren't all the way exclusive, so it was okay for him to talk to other chicks. However, that didn't mean my feelings weren't hurt whenever he told me about some new bitch.

On some real shit, that was one of the main reasons why I had ended up messing with Jerome. Prior to finding out about his secret son and him fucking Mya, I low key envied his and JaNair's relationship a little bit. How he loved her and treated her was the same way I wished Lil Ray would treat me. Then it didn't help that Jerome was my accomplice the night I went to check out that bitch Diamond at her place of employment. Jay was busy with classes and couldn't go, so she sent him instead. We all partied from time to time, so it wasn't out of the norm for him and me to kick it. The night that we went to the strip club, we got so drunk while shooting pool and having a good time that we slipped up and kissed while sitting in my car. One thing led to another, and next thing I knew, I was riding the fuck out of his dick in the passenger seat. I knew we should've ended whatever that was that happened between us there, but for some strange reason, we kept the shenanigans going and ended up losing the one person who mattered most to both of us . . . JaNair.

My mom placing a whiny Aspen in my lap snapped me from my trip down memory lane. "I'll be back in an hour or two. Make sure you lock up if you go somewhere."

I took my milk-filled titties out of my bra and began to breastfeed Aspen. "I'm not going anywhere today. I'ma just lounge around and clean up a little. Plus, Lil Ray is coming over after he gets off work."

"Oh yeah?" She smiled. "Is he staying over tonight? If so, text me and let me know while I'm out so that I can pick up a few things for dinner."

I nodded my head.

"Don't forget about the mail. It's on the table in the dining room, okay!"

After my mom left, I finished feeding my beautiful baby girl, then put her to sleep. For the next forty-five minutes or so, I cleaned up my room, the nursery, took the trash out, and washed the little bit of dishes that were in the sink. By the time I finished all of that and folded all the new baby clothes my mother had just bought for Aspen, I was a little tired. Thinking I could get in a quick nap before she woke up, I headed to my room in search of my bed but turned around when the rumbling in my stomach reminded me that I hadn't eaten anything all day. After going back to the kitchen, I made a turkey sandwich, grabbed a few handfuls of chips, a bottle of water, and went into the dining room.

The mail my mother had told me about was neatly stacked in the middle of the table, with colored envelopes on top. After taking a few bites of my sandwich and satisfying my hunger, I went through the stack. Because of my now A1 credit, a lot of banks were sending me shit for credit cards, so the majority of the letters were from them. I continued to go through my mail. Finding nothing important, I was about to toss the whole stack in the trash, but I stopped dead in my tracks when the DNA Matrix logo in the top left-hand corner of the last envelope made my whole body freeze. The paternity results were finally here, and I didn't know whether I wanted to be relieved or nervous.

I sat and stared at the envelope for what seemed like hours before I got the courage to rip the sucka open. The nerves in my body were going crazy during the time my eyes scanned the letter for what I wanted to know.

"Oh . . . my . . . God!" The words slipped from my mouth as I was finally given the answer to the question of which man had fathered my child.

Without even thinking, I went straight to the nursery, placed a sleeping Aspen in her Carkoon, grabbed my keys, purse, and diaper bag, and headed out the door.

I knew I had told my mom I wasn't going anywhere, but I needed to pay my baby daddy a visit and see where his head was at before all hell broke loose.

"LaLa?" my sister said after opening the door I was just about to knock on.

"Niecey?" My facial expression was just as confused as hers.

"What the hell are you doing here?" we asked at the same time.

"I, uh . . . I . . . uh—" Niecey was stumbling over her words, which meant she was about to lie about something, so I cut her off.

"You know what? It's none of my business, so I don't even care." I looked into a set of eyes that were identical to mine. "I know I may be the last person you want to be giving you any type of advice, but, Niecey, make sure whatever feelings you're still harboring for my baby daddy don't mess up the great relationship you're trying to build with Toby."

Her face scrunched up. "It's not even like . . . Wait a minute . . . Did you just say your baby daddy?" The hurt look on her face literally tore my heart into pieces. We may have been beefing at the moment, but Niecey was still my sister, my twin sister at that, so I was feeling everything she was right now. I handed her the test results letter. I never wanted to hurt my sister or JaNair like I did, but it was too late to change anything now.

"Who are you talking to, Niecey?" Big Will asked when he finally came to the door.

Niecey looked at me with misty eyes, then down at Aspen, sleeping soundly in her seat, then back up to me again.

"Apparently, I'm talking to the mother of your child," she said, stepping fully out of the house, tears coming from her eyes. "I can't believe my niece belongs to you. Ten years . . . I gave you ten years of my life, and not once have you ever given me something so precious." She bit her bottom lip. "But you know what, Will . . . ? Like I said a few minutes ago, thank you for fucking up so royally this time. If you and my sister had never fucked, I probably wouldn't have given Toby a chance, so in actuality, I'm thankful to the both of you."

She looked at me, then back at Will. "I hope you're a better father figure to my niece than you were a boyfriend to me. And just so we're clear, let me reiterate what we just discussed in your home. Please don't call, text, email, or social media me anymore. You and I are over and will *never* be together again. Now, if you two will excuse me, I need to get home to my man."

"That white boy will never love you like I do," Will yelled at Niecey's retreating back. "When you get tired of that little pink dick, you'll be back," he added, but by then Niecey was in her car and was already pulling off.

I watched as a range of emotions crossed his face. He went from mad, to sad, to desolate in a matter of seconds. When I saw what I thought looked like a single tear fall from his eye, Will turned his head in the opposite direction and tried to discreetly wipe away any traces of it. Right now probably wasn't the best time to bring up my reason for being here, but Will had already missed out on the first few months of his child's life.

"Look, Will, we need to talk."

"About what?" he snapped, looking in the direction Niecey had just driven off in.

"Um . . . Aspen . . . our daughter. Didn't you hear what my sister just said?"

He turned his heated gaze to me. Those copper-colored eyes, which normally had the girls going crazy, were dark and filled with hate.

"Yeah, I heard what she said, but ask me if I give a fuck." He shook his head and laughed. "Me fucking you was the worst mistake of my life, and I really don't wanna have shit to do with you or *your* baby. I'm not coming out of the pocket, watching, or bonding with anything that didn't come out of your sister's pussy. If you want support from me, take me to court, bitch, because other than that, you ain't getting shit." He looked down at Aspen, then back at me with a scowl before going into his apartment and slamming the door in my face. The minute the loud noise hit her ears, Aspen woke up and started screaming at the top of her lungs.

"Shhh, baby. It's okay . . . shh," I said, trying to soothe her back to sleep. "Everything is going to be all right."

I tried to keep the tears threatening to fall at bay but had no such luck. Then, to make matters worse, Lil Ray was now calling my phone. Rather than answering the call, I just sent a quick text telling him that I had a few errands to run, and I'd meet him at his house instead.

The text he had sent earlier crossed my mind; we definitely needed to talk now. Hopefully, all things would work out for the best in Aspen's case, and Lil Ray's feelings of being her only father wouldn't change. If not, and he decided that this was too much for him to handle right now, at least I still had my mama.

Semaj

"Hey, Auntie. What's up?"

"Nothing, nephew. But why are you whispering?"

I laughed. My aunt was too nosey for her own good. "Because JaNair's still asleep, and I don't wanna wake her up."

"Boy, it's ten o'clock in the morning out here, which means it's noon there. Tell that girl to wake her ass up before she sleeps the day away."

I laughed. "I would, Auntie, but we, uh . . . we kinda had a long night last night and this morning." Just thinking about the snug juiciness between JaNair's thighs had my dick hard as fuck and ready to go again.

"Uh-huh. You just make sure you come up for air long enough to make it back in time for the baby shower barbecue next weekend. You know RayShaun will have a fit if you aren't here. Besides, you've been in Texas long enough. It's time for you and my niece-in-law to come back to California."

My auntie Shirley was a trip, and I loved her for it. When I'd told her about JaNair and me finally doing the do, she'd been more excited than me. She'd even started picking out baby names for her future grandbabies and shit. I'd had to tell her to slow down for a minute. Although I may have pumped a few babies inside JaNair already, there were some things we still needed to get through. One being that fuck boy Jerome.

That nigga called JaNair's phone so much, it was annoying. She called herself being slick by turning the ringer off so I wouldn't hear it, but what she should've done was turn that muthafucka completely off so that I couldn't see her screen still lighting up every five minutes. Between him and Mya, I didn't know who called the most. I had tried to get her to change her number a couple times, but every time I brought it up, she always gave me the excuse of needing to check her voice messages before she did. It had been a week since we last talked about the shit, and her number was still the same.

A few times while she was asleep, I answered her phone when I saw his name pop up on the screen. The first couple of times he just hung up, but lately he'd been saying little slick shit to get under my skin, like he did last night.

"What's up with it?" I answered, only to get complete silence. "Hello? Caller, are you there?" I asked a few seconds later.

"Put my girl on the phone." He tried to put some bass in his voice, but the nigga failed miserably.

"Why do you keep calling this number, looking for your girl? Last time I checked, this line belonged to mine."

"JaNair will never be with you. A damn near thirty-year-old nigga living in his aunt's garage, trying to be the next Scott Storch?" he said, slurring. He laughed at his own joke. "You might be able to pull Mya's ho ass with your pathetic life, but not my JaNair."

"I think she stopped being your JaNair the minute she dismissed your proposal and hopped on a plane all the way to Texas to be with me."

"Fuck you! You snake-headed muthafucka."

"Unfortunately for you, I don't swing that way. But I promise to do just that to JaNair as soon as she wakes up."

I laughed as that nigga started going crazy, yelling and shit, telling me that I better not touch his Jay. I almost felt sorry for the dude but changed my mind when a thick and smooth caramel thigh slid across my leg. The heat radiating from Jay's pussy had my body reacting instantly and my dick standing straight up. Jerome was still slurring and screeching at the top of his lungs when I ended the call. I wasn't worried about that nigga or anything else he had to say at that moment, though. JaNair's scent had my attention, and I just had to get me a taste.

Even though that nigga had been drunk when he called last night, I wasn't about to let all the disrespectful shit he'd said pass. As soon as I caught up with him in the city, which I knew would be soon, I was going to beat his ass.

"Have you talked to Tasha yet?" my aunt asked, and my head instantly started to hurt. Since I'd been out here in Texas, her ass had been getting real slick at the mouth with my auntie and she'd been getting really out of line whenever she went by the house.

I didn't know if she was showing off for that new nigga she was fucking with or if she was in her feelings because Jay was out here with me. Whatever the case may be, she was really tripping out and was not allowing me to speak with my daughter. Then the couple of times I had tried to have her come out and visit me for a weekend or two, she had taken the plane ticket I bought and had cashed it in.

I ignored my aunt's question and talked to her for a few more minutes before getting off the phone and hopping in the shower. When I got out fifteen minutes later, JaNair's ass was still asleep, but she wasn't going to be for long. The way her round ass was peeking out from underneath the little shirt she was wearing had me rocked up again.

After dropping on the floor the towel that was wrapped around my waist, I pounced on her ass the second she turned onto her back. Whatever she was dreaming about already had her pussy super wet and ready for me to slide right in.

As soon as my dick hit her cervix, my mans was rewarded with a tsunami of her sweet essence. My stomach and thighs were drenched with her cum, and I wanted to get wet again.

JaNair's eyes popped open as soon as I slid into her again, and the sexiest moan escaped her lips.

"What . . . the . . . fuck, Semaj! Ahhh!" she screamed, cumming again.

I wasn't trying to bust anytime soon, but the way that her pussy was vibrating and splashing on my dick had my nuts tightening up and ready to explode.

"Semaj . . . you . . . um!" She closed her eyes and bit her lip. I promise the sex faces she made would make the strongest man weak.

"I what, baby?"

"Fuck!" she moaned. "You . . . you . . . better . . ."

"I better what?" I asked as I sucked her bottom lip into my mouth. The sweet taste of peaches invaded my taste buds.

JaNair never answered my question. Instead, she locked her legs around my waist, pushed up on her elbows, and then flipped us over in one quick motion. Our bodies were still connected to each other as she continued to rock her hips to my thrusts.

"Fuck, baby!" It was my turn to cry out, and I had a good reason. The way JaNair started flexing her muscles and bouncing on my shit was all it took for me to completely come undone. I grabbed her hips and power drove into her pussy until my kids were decorating every inch of her walls.

She collapsed onto my chest, and we both lay there for a few seconds, talking with the beat of our hearts.

Her phone, which was on the nightstand, started to vibrate, interrupting our little intimate moment.

"Yo, when you gonna change your number?"

She sat up and looked at me, those cocoa-brown eyes low but still sexy as fuck.

"I will, babe. I just need to go through my voicemail."

I ran my fingers through my dreads and closed my eyes. It was the only thing I could do to calm myself and keep myself from going off on her ass.

"Jay, that doesn't take but ten minutes, fifteen tops. You've had a whole week to listen to that shit. What you waiting for, baby?"

I knew she could tell by the look on my face that I was getting upset. She tried to distract me by kissing different spots on my face and licking on my neck, but I wasn't falling for that shit. When she finally realized that that wasn't working, she decided to give me an answer.

"Honestly, Semaj." She shrugged her shoulders. "I don't know."

I grunted and shook my head. She couldn't really be serious, could she? "Naw, Jay, you know why. You just don't want to admit it."

She smacked her lips.

We sat in silence for a few minutes, me staring at her and her staring at me. When she got tired of the awkward silence, she tried to dismount off me, but I grabbed her hips and stopped her from moving.

"You know I'm not with that 'run off' bullshit, so knock it off. Look at me, Jay." It took her a couple of seconds, but she finally turned her eyes to mine. "I'ma give you until we fly home next weekend to change your number." I pointed at myself and then her. "After that, I can't promise where we will be if it's not taken care of. As much as I don't want it to happen, I also know that you may have to see that nigga to return some of his shit and get yours. I trust you, so I don't have a problem with you seeing him one last time. But once that happens, you need to shut down any and everything that nigga tries to throw you. I'm willing to take this ride with you, but I will not be made a fool of for a muthafucka that didn't love you in the first place, you feel me?"

She nodded her head.

"You also need to understand that you can't start the next chapter of your life if you keep reading the last one, Jay," I added.

"I understand, and I heard everything you just said."

"For the sake of this relationship, I hope you do," I said before grabbing the back of her neck and bringing her soft, pouty lips down to mine.

After having sex again and taking a shower together, we ate the leftover food we had from Brennan's the other night and took a nap. Avantae's party was in a few hours, and I wanted to be nice and refreshed for what was in store. The song I did with Killa Mike was going to be dropping for the whole city to hear, and with this party being as star studded as Tae said it would be, I had no doubt that my line would get hit up to do a few tracks with some of the heavyweights in the game. I was well on my way to being the super producer that I'd always dreamed I'd be, as well as being able to provide a nice life for me, my family, and now JaNair.

Mya

Man, when I tell you that your girl was back to stunting on these bitches, I mean it. I still had my little bucket to drive around in, but I was working on changing that. With a place to now lay my head and a constant flow of cash coming in, I was on my way back to being the fly and fierce Mya. My hair was laid, my nails were done, and my body was looking right, especially in the skintight Paige denim jeans I had on. Of course, the Trina Turk top that I was wearing fit a little looser than I liked, but that was okay. Pretending to be pregnant did have its drawbacks when it came to my wardrobe, but as long as I was getting this money, I really didn't mind.

Besides, the focal point of my outfit today was the pink Alexander McQueen block boots I'd received as an early "push" gift from Cassan last week. Thanks to his pussy-whipped ass, I'd been back on top and doing better than before, and like I'd told that dumbass wife of his the day my other car got repoed, Cassan would never stop fucking with me. Yeah, it had taken a little time to get back to where we were after she came back into the picture, but he'd made up for it by replacing everything she had destroyed as well as giving me a few things that I'd always wanted. Like a trip to Cozumel, Mexico, which we would be taking in a few weeks. The nigga had paid for my passport to be expedited and everything. I had even got him to buy me a whole new wardrobe for the trip. I was in heaven, all thanks to planting that fake pregnancy seed in his head, and wasn't nobody, not even his wife, gonna stop shit.

The day after I left Ryan's house empty handed. I didn't know what I was going to do. Jerome had blocked my calls, JaNair still wasn't answering her phone, and Niecey had flat out told me to fuck off. I was sitting in the parking lot at Costco, eating a hot dog, when my phone started ringing back-to-back. Because I didn't know the number, I let the call go to voicemail several times, but after about the seventh call, I said fuck it and decided to answer the phone.

To my surprise, it was Cassan calling to apologize for how everything had gone down and asked how I was doing. After putting on the waterworks and informing him about the bundle of joy we would be having soon, I was instructed to meet him at some townhome community in Century City. I tried to get him to come to me so that I could hit him up for the money I needed for an abortion, grab a few more hot dogs, then go to the motel I was staying at and pay them for another two weeks, but he had a different plan. So with the last couple of dollars I had in my purse, I gassed up my Honda and drove to the address he gave me.

"Who lives here?" I asked as he showed me around the two-story, three-bedroom, two-bath home, which was already furnished. The appliances and electronics were all up to date, but the blinds, carpeting, and kitchen really needed a facelift.

"You . . . if you want it."

I looked at him like he was crazy. "How will I do that without a job or any source of income, Cassan? You see, I had to go back to driving my first car because I was behind on the payments for my other one."

He stopped in his tracks and turned to me. A serious look was on his handsome face. I wanted to drop to my knees and break him off like I used to, but I needed to see where this situation was heading.

"Mya, I'm not about to have you or my baby sleeping in raggedy motels and living off of hot dogs and free cups of water when I have the means to do something about it."

Shit, I wasn't expecting none of this to happen, especially when all I wanted was a few notes to hold me over until I was able to move back in with JaNair or find another sucka to trap. It wasn't like I was really pregnant, anyway. If I did take him up on his offer, what would he say a couple of months from now, when my belly was still flat? Man, who was I kidding? I wasn't about pass up this opportunity. I'd just have to come up with some other plan when that time came. I was more than likely going to take Cassan up on his offer, but not before we hashed out a couple of things.

"And where does your wife fit into all of this? Does she know about this house?"

He shook his head. "Naw, she doesn't. I purchased this property before I ever met her. I bought it for my mama, but she didn't want to live out this way, so I just started renting it out to make a little extra money. I was going to put it on the market, but since you need somewhere to stay, I'll let you live here . . . rent free, of course. I'ma take care of you and the baby."

Rent free . . . I liked the sound of that. I walked back into the living room and sat down on the plush leather couch. That muthafucka was so soft and comfy, I almost fainted.

"So where does that put us? Are we living together again?" I said.

"Eventually, we will. Right now, though, I have to square away a few things with my wife to make sure we're good. Then, by the time the baby gets here, *everything should be cool," he said as he came and sat down next to me and placed his hand on my belly. It was a good thing I had just eaten those two hot dogs, or the little bulge in my belly would have been nonexistent.*

On that day, my and Cassan's relationship basically picked up right where we had left off. The only difference was instead of seeing him every day like before, I saw him every two days. Sometimes he'd spend the night; other times he'd leave before ten in the evening. I wasn't tripping off that shit, though. I understood he had to divide his time between the wife and me. As long as he continued to take care of me like he had said he would, I really didn't care where he laid his head.

"Okay, ma'am. Your total is forty-two, seventy-one."

I gave the cashier my new debit card to slide and started placing my bags into the basket. I had come to Target today to buy a few baby magazines and toys, whatever I needed to make it seem like I was really about to have his baby. I wouldn't have to do this shit for long, though, because I had come up with a foolproof plan. On one of the days when Cassan didn't come over at all, I was going to, unfortunately, have a miscarriage. I figured I'd take some of the money I'd been saving and get a hotel room for a few days. Turn off my phone and avoid going on social media for a while. That nigga was going to go crazy looking for me and wondering about the baby. I'd return on the weekend, totally distraught, upset, and on bed rest. When he questioned me about my whereabouts, that was when I was going to tell him about losing the baby and being in the hospital all alone.

There was no way in the world this wouldn't work. His heart was going to literally break when I told him that. Cassan was already in love with the baby he thought was there.

"Can you enter your pin and press the green button, please?" the cashier asked.

I entered four-five-five-two, which was the town house's security code, and pressed the button. A piece of paper came out of the register, and the cashier tore it off.

"Can I see the card again? It's saying you entered the wrong pin number."

I gave her the card, and she slid it again. I typed in the pin, then pressed the button.

"I'm sorry, ma'am. Do you wanna try it as a credit? Because it's saying the same thing again."

Instead of holding the line up any longer, I did the transaction as a credit, showed her my driver's license, signed the receipt, and then went on my way.

"I'ma curse that muthafucka out when he comes over tonight," I said as I pulled into traffic. Why would he change the pin number and not tell me? That was so embarrassing. It was a good thing the card had my name on it, or else it really would've been a problem.

I did want to stop at a few more stores but decided not to. I didn't wanna chance having the card declined this again, so I went home.

When I pulled up to the house, Cassan's car was already in the driveway. With it being Friday, I'd figured he was here already. He always worked half a day, then came to spend the rest of the afternoon with me, since the weekend was reserved for wifey.

"Baby, where are you?" I yelled out as I walked through the front door. "Can you come and help me with the bags?"

When I didn't receive a reply, I looked around the living room, in search of some of his shit, and a couple things struck me as kind of odd. The oil-stained boots he wore to work every day weren't in the corner by the door, like they always were whenever he came over. The magazines and mail, which I normally left all over the place, were still in the same spots I had left them, whereas

Cassan's neat freak ass would've put them back in their rightful place. Even the glass of water I had had earlier was still sitting on the coffee table, without a coaster underneath, so something was up.

"Cassan!" I called out, but there was still no answer. I dropped all the bags that I was holding in the living room and started to make my way upstairs, to the master suite. If his ass was in there, lying across my new duvet with those dirty-ass boots on, watching ESPN, I was about to go off.

As I got closer to the bedroom, the nasty stench of cigarette smoke invaded my nose. *This nigga better not be in my shit.* I hated the smell of cigarettes on my clothes.

For some reason, a funny feeling washed over me, but I ignored it, like all the other times before. When you did so much dirt in your life, you tended to get that feeling a lot, but for me, nothing had ever happened.

"Cassan, I know good and gosh damn well you ain't in this room, smoking around my clothes. You know how I hate . . . ," I said but trailed off when I opened the door to my bedroom and saw what was before me.

All my new clothes, shoes, jewelry, and purses were piled up in the middle of the king-size bed, soaked in what I now realized was lighter fluid. I looked around the rest of the room in horror at the way everything had been run through. Dresser drawers had been emptied out, and their contents thrown on the floor. My vanity mirror was cracked and turned over. The makeup that I had just purchased from MAC had been used to write all kinds of nasty shit on the wall. Even the vibrators and sex toys I broke out on special occasions had been broken in half or destroyed.

"Cassan!" I yelled. "What the fuck!" These were all the clothes I had to my name, new and old. He was most definitely going to replace all this shit, but not before I got off in his ass.

The door to the bathroom in our bedroom was open, and I was more than ready for this fight to go down, but when the last person I expected to see waltzed out of that muthafucka, with a cigarette hanging from her lips and my new red satin La Perla bra on, I almost passed out.

"Didn't think you'd see me today, huh?" she asked as she walked farther into the room. "I didn't think so, either, but when that husband of mine slipped up a few days ago and said some crazy shit while we were arguing, I didn't have any other choice but to check into some shit for myself."

She sat down on the edge of the bed and picked a lighter up from off the floor.

Then she went on. "You know, I distinctly remember telling you to stay the fuck away from Cassan the last time we saw each other. I see now that you're the type of bitch that needs to be shown something better than told it."

I opened my mouth but didn't say anything. For the first time in my life, I was starting to regret not taking heed of her previous warnings. The cold look in her eyes told me that she wasn't here to talk at all. She lit the cigarette, with her penetrating gaze on me. After taking a few puffs, she closed her eyes and let her head fall back as she blew a thick cloud of smoke from her mouth.

"I hear you're supposed to be pregnant. Is that true?" She wasn't even looking at me as she spoke, just kept her eyes trained on the fake sonogram picture I had in a crystal frame on the nightstand.

"Uh . . . I . . . I . . ."

"Choose wisely now. You already got one strike against you for not listening. You don't wanna know what happens when you have two."

I thought about lying, because who in their right mind would hurt a pregnant woman? Then again, I didn't want to be on the receiving end of whatever happened after the second strike. So like a good little girl, I decided to tell the truth.

"I'm . . . uh . . . I'm not . . . pregnant," I admitted, my voice dropping a few octaves.

We sat in silence for a few minutes before she turned her heated gaze toward me. I wanted to know what she was thinking, because the blank stare on her face was throwing me off. When she started shaking her head and laughing real loud a few seconds later, though, I knew I needed to get my ass up out of this house.

"I can't believe that dumb muthafucka fell for the oldest trick in the book," she said between laughs. "And the nigga went all out too." She pulled on one of the bra straps. "Buying fancy lingerie and shit. All for a bitch who's not even pregnant with his baby." She laughed so hard and long after saying that, that I joined in on the laughter.

"What you laughing at?" she asked, finally calming down.

"You."

She completely stopped laughing and licked her lips. The cold look was back in her eyes. "Oh yeah?"

I nodded my head, then quickly shook it no. Maybe laughing with her crazy ass wasn't such a good idea. *Oh shit!* Did she think I was laughing at her? Before I even got the chance to explain, I felt the worst pain across my face.

"What the fuck!" I yelled as I tried to shield myself, but my hands were knocked down to my sides.

Two more slashes were made. Then a fourth, then a fifth. I fell down to the floor, with my sight totally gone. Every time I tried to rub away the wetness blocking my vision, my whole face would burn. I could tell by the copper taste in my mouth that I was bleeding. Just how bad, I didn't know.

"I hope every time you look in the mirror once that cute little face of yours heals up, you are reminded to stay your ass away from married men or men who are already involved, because the next bitch might not be so nice." Although I couldn't see the smile I knew she had on her face, I could hear it loud and clear in her voice.

"What have you done to my face?" I cried out, still trying to open my eyes.

"Nothing too bad. Just a little facial reconstruction. Why are you tripping? When I was in jail, I heard this shit was all the rage in Cali. You didn't even have to pay for yours. I did that shit for free."

I tried to get up but failed miserably. The last thing I remembered before totally blacking out was my eyes finally opening and seeing Cassan's crazy-ass wife flicking the new cigarette she had just lit onto my lighter fluid–drenched clothes. Flames shot up to the ceiling immediately, and smoke started to fill the room. I prayed to God that help would come for me some kind of way. If not, I hoped it was not too late to repent for my past transgressions and make peace with my soul.

JaNair

I ain't gotta tell you why I do it
Get cash, get cars, go hard
I ain't gotta tell you why I do it
Nigga, I don't ask why you do your job
I ain't gotta tell you why I do it
I grind sundown to sunrise
Don't tell me to prove it, 'cause I might lose it
I ain't gotta tell you why I do it

August Alsina's "Why I Do It" was blaring through the speakers as we passed through the front door of 5th Amendment Bar.

"That doorman was cute as hell. You know I like me a big, black country-ass nigga," Neesh screamed into my ear.

I shook my head at her crazy ass and kept walking through the large crowd.

"Did Semaj tell you where they would be? I texted him before we came in, but he never responded," she yelled.

I stopped in my tracks and looked around the swanky club and took in its live scenery. As tall as Semaj's ass was, you would think I'd be able to spot him in this crowded-ass club, but there were so many people blocking my vision with their drinks and hands in the air, I couldn't see anything. Maybe I should've gone home and ridden up here with him, instead of staying at Neesh's house and getting dressed there after she finished doing my hair.

"Excuse me . . . ," Neesh said to the big security guard whom I didn't even notice standing behind us. "Can you please point us in the direction of Big Tae's party?"

The security guard looked Neesh up and down, then turned his attention to me and did the same. He licked his lips and eyed us once more before he pushed himself off the black wall and started walking toward the middle of the dance floor.

"Damn! Niggas in Texas are rude as fuck," I muttered.

"Naw, it isn't all niggas," Neesh said. "Just his big Terry Crews–looking ass. I wonder if he has a girlfriend."

"Girl, sit your horny self down somewhere." I laughed as I went into my purse and pulled out my cell phone. "I'm about to call Semaj. It's too many damn people in here to be trying to play hide-and-seek with his ass."

Before I could scroll down to Semaj's name, the security guard came back up to us.

"Why y'all still standing here?" His accent was way thicker than Neesh's, and he spoke much slower. "I had to walk back through that big-ass crowd to come back and get y'all. Niggas stepping on my shoes and shit." I looked down at his all-black Air Force Ones.

"How were we supposed to know to follow you if you ain't say shit to us?" Neesh replied. "Hell, for all we know, you could be some type of serial killer or something."

He smirked at Neesh. "The only thing I'd kill is that pussy if you let me," he responded. That shut her ass up real quick. "But we can save that conversation for another day. Now, if you follow me, I'll take you to where you need to be." Turning on his heel, he didn't say another word as he grabbed ahold of Neesh's hand, and she grabbed mine. We walked back to the jumping dance floor and passed the busy Vegas-style bar, then stopped in front of a roped-off flight of stairs.

"Tae's party is up there." The security guard pointed with his head. "Now, you two enjoy yourselves, and don't forget to give me your number before you leave, sexy."

"Why wait until before we leave? You can have it now," Neesh said, flirting, as she offered him her business card.

I rolled my eyes and shook my head. This girl stayed pulling niggas.

He took her card with a nod, then removed the rope. I didn't know why, but for some reason, I became a little nervous as we started walking up the short flight of stairs. Semaj hadn't seen me damn near all day, and I was hoping my new look didn't come as too much of a surprise to him. I looked down at the Bao Tranchi–inspired LBD that I was rocking. It wasn't an exact replica of the one Jennifer Lopez wore for her forty-sixth birthday, but it was damn near close. Although a bit revealing, I loved the way it showed parts of my body and hugged all my curves. I'd paired it with some purple Nicholas Kirkwood suede and mesh T-strap pumps and a purple envelope clutch. In this outfit, I was ready to represent for my man and enjoy the night.

As I walked up the stairs, Neesh on my heels, I kept touching the back of my head because I was still trying to get used to my new length. Neesh swatted my hand down.

"If you keep smoothing your hair down like that, you're going to make it flat. Stop being nervous. Like I told you earlier, Semaj is going to love it. You see how all these other niggas can't keep their eyes off of you."

"I just hope he likes my hair. I don't know what I was thinking when I let you cut it and put this multicolored bob in my shit."

Neesh smacked her lips. "Girl, please. That style and color looks good on you. There aren't too many people who could rock the colors red and purple on their head and get away with it. Not only do the colors go with your skin tone, but the way I slayed and styled that bob has you looking all kinds of sexy."

I smiled and nodded my head in agreement, then pushed farther up to the VIP section, with Neesh close behind me.

"I sho' hope Semaj knows how to fight," she said and snickered in my ear as the majority of the men that were standing around with drinks in their hands, socializing, turned their lustful gazes toward us.

I didn't know why Neesh thought everybody was looking only at me. She was turning heads, too, with the black sequin booty shorts and halter bra she was wearing. Her stomach was a little pudgy, and she had a couple of rolls in her back, but she still looked good. The short sleeve tuxedo jacket she had put on over her outfit hid her chubbiness but put a huge spotlight on her ample amount of cleavage. With her face beat to the gawds and a jet-black, bone-straight weave parted down the middle, Neesh was giving me and these men up her all kinds of life.

Ignoring the catcalling and stares, I scanned the crowd for Semaj. With everyone in all black and the VIP section being so thick, it was hard for me to spot him at first. That was until my eyes ran across Kwency's "not complying with the dress code" ho ass.

This was supposed to be an all-black party, but in true ho fashion, the bitch was trying to stand out with the hot pink, sleeveless, body-con dress she had on and that bright red messy bun she had on the top of her head. I was not a hater or anything, so I was not gone sit here and act like the dress didn't look good on her curvy body, but the bitch was on my shit list right now, so she'd never hear that compliment from me.

"I swear I hate that bitch," Neesh said as she stood next to me, eyeing her sister. "Always wants to be the center of attention, but stays getting her ass beat, fucking with a nigga that don't belong to her."

I watched as Kwency slid her hand down Semaj's arm and laughed at whatever he had just said. Because this was somewhat of a networking thing for him, I was gonna try my best not to show my ass tonight. However, when it came to this bitch, things could most definitely change.

"Excuse me, shawty." said a deep, raspy voice in my ear from behind me. "I'm not trying to be rude, but you're working the hell out of this dress, Mama." He was so close up on my ass that I could feel his semi-erect dick brush against it a couple of times.

"You're not being rude, and thank you for the compliment," I said, taking a step forward.

I felt his hand lightly touch the small of my back. "Well, in that case, let's head on over to the bar so that I can get you something to drink and we can get to know each other a little better."

Before I could turn around and open my mouth to decline the offer myself, a familiar voice did it for me instead. "Naw, she good, bruh . . . on getting to know you and them drinks."

My wide eyes connected with Semaj's, and butterflies started to dance around in my belly. He snaked his arm around me in a possessive manner and pulled me into his chest. The Bond No. 9 Riverside Drive cologne he had on automatically had my body reacting to his scent. The sexy smirk on his lips turned into a seductive smile when he felt my hard nipples pressing against his chest. By the appreciative glance he gave my body, I could tell he was feeling my dress and new look.

We were so lost in each other's arms that we forgot ole boy was still standing there.

"My bad, man. I didn't know she was with you," he said, grabbing our attention.

Semaj nodded his head, then nuzzled his face in the crook of my neck, inhaling my scent, before he placed a trail of kisses all the way up to my mouth. As soon as our lips connected, our bodies seemed to unite in a way I hadn't experienced before.

"Damn," we both said breathlessly as we finally pulled apart from each other.

Semaj licked his lips. "What took you so long to get here? I tried to call your phone a couple times to make sure y'all was good at the door, but I kept getting some automated system."

"That's because . . . I changed my number today."

"Oh yeah?"

I nodded my head.

"Why is that?"

"Because I told you I was."

He looked at me with raised eyebrows.

I went on. "And . . . because I heard everything you were saying to me the other night about starting new chapters and whatnot." I wrapped my arms around his neck. "I really wanna give whatever this is that we have going on between us a fair chance, Semaj. And I understand that I can't do that if Jerome is still blowing my phone up and causing some unnecessary waves between us."

He nodded his head. "So you sure you over fuck boy?"

I thought about his question for a minute, then nodded my head yes.

"How do you know?" he asked.

"Honestly? Because while I was listening to my voice-mail, I heard a conversation between LaLa and Jerome that I don't think they knew was being recorded. Not only did I find out that they had sex more than once, but I also found out that he fucked my cousin as well."

His eyes got big. "Wait a minute! Your cousin, as in Mya?"

"The one and only. Funny thing is, after hearing all of that, I wasn't mad at Mya or LaLa anymore. I was actually mad at myself for putting up with Jerome's bullshit for so long and for opening my heart up to a nigga who clearly didn't deserve it."

"So what you saying?"

I thought back to what Semaj had said to me the day we stood between our houses after we shared our first kiss.

"The ball is in your court . . . Whenever you ready to let a real nigga show you how a queen should be treated, you know where to find me. Both doors will always be open for you."

"I'm saying . . . I'm ready to pass the ball from my court to you, and if the offer still stands to let a real nigga show me how a queen is supposed to be treated, I want to experience that too."

He stared into my eyes for a long time before he bent over and pressed his lips against mine. When he slid his tongue into my mouth, I literally melted against him. For some reason, this kiss felt kind of different, as if he'd been holding back when our tongues tangled before. The kiss we were sharing right now was filled with so much passion that my head grew light.

"I love you, JaNair," I heard Semaj say when we ended the kiss. Even with the music playing loud as hell, I still heard what he said. "And you don't ever have to worry about me hurting you. All I ask is that you give us a chance, and I promise that you will never want for anything."

If I wasn't light headed before, then I fo' sure was now, and enjoying every minute of it. I now knew why that kiss felt so different. It was filled with love. A love that I would have no problem returning.

We kissed again, and when Semaj deepened our kiss, it was only second nature for him to cup my ass and pull me up to straddle his waist. With my dress bunched up and stretched to the max, I started grinding on his dick. I needed to feel him buried deep inside me, and I wanted to feel him now. It took Neesh clearing her throat for us to remember that we were in a public place and not the privacy of his home. After a few more seconds of kissing, Semaj slowly put me down, and I fixed my clothes.

"Damn! I leave to get me a drink from the bar and come back to the two of you damn near about to fuck in VIP," Neesh said.

She never received a response. Semaj and I were staring so intensely at one another, still high off our lip-lock, that her joke flew completely over our heads.

"Ook. Uh, Jay, I'ma be on the dance floor if you need me. If you two decide to dip out while I'm gone, just shoot me a text, so I know." She looked between us for confirmation. When I slowly nodded my head, she turned away and headed out of the VIP.

Finally taking my eyes off Semaj, I watched as Neesh pushed her way through the large crowd and walked right up to the security guard we had spoken to earlier. The big-ass grin on his face told me that he was just as happy to see her again as she was to see him.

A light tap on my ass had me turning back around. Semaj was now back in my personal space and staring at me again.

"You ready to get out of here?"

"What about the party?" I said.

"I already made a few connections before you got here. If anybody else wants to get at me, I'm sure they can holla at Tae. That nigga knows everybody."

We ended up leaving the club about an hour later, after a few rounds of toasting and goodbyes. Ironically, I didn't have to check Kwency at all tonight, even after she tried to sashay her ass all up in Semaj's face, introducing him to some bigwigs in the business. Before she got too carried away with all that touchy-feely shit, Semaj shut that ass down in front of everybody, embarrassing the hell out of her. Then, if that wasn't enough, the whole VIP had a laughing fit at her expense when the wife of one of the bigwigs beat her ass and poured a whole bottle of champagne on her. Come to find out, she had fucked the husband in one of the club's bathrooms earlier and thought no one knew. Poor little tink-tink.

Anyhoo . . .

After Semaj and I got home, you already know we made love in and on every square inch of the condo. By the time we finished loving on each other, we were totally exhausted and in need of some serious sleep. It was going on five in the morning, and the sun was starting to rise on the horizon. A beautiful sky-blue tint was decorating the sky, and the tiny rays of sunlight were spilling through the blinds.

I could tell by the way Semaj's chest was slowly moving up and down that he was on his way to sleep, but before he went, I wanted to make sure he was really ready for what we were getting into. I didn't have a hard time getting over Jerome, because I now saw that the love I had for him wasn't as real as the love I felt for Semaj. I probably would die if Semaj ever did me like Jerome.

"Hey . . ." I pulled lightly on one of his dreads. "You still up?"

Semaj rolled over onto his side so that he was facing me. Eyes super low, but not all the way closed. The lavender oil he used on his dreads lingered on the spot on the pillow he had just moved his head from. His smooth milk-chocolate skin glistened from the small rays of the sun that illuminated the bed. I swear I could wake up to this vision every morning for the rest of my life. I just hoped he felt the same way.

"Yeah. What's up?" His voice was a little groggy and deeper than usual, so I knew he would be out at any minute.

"I just wanted you to know that I really appreciate everything you've done for me. From being a listening ear to a shoulder to cry on, my weed-smoking partner, and my escape plan when I needed to get away from that mess back at home. It was like you knew what I needed, and I never had to tell you anything. You took care of me after that accident and made sure I was good. You even helped me out with things that you didn't have to, like those bills Mya forgot to pay. You did all of that knowing that I had a man, and not once did you ever try to push up on me or break us apart. It was like you were waiting for me to see your worth, and now that I finally see it, you wanna give me the world."

He kissed me on my nose, then wiped away the tear I didn't even know I had on my cheek.

I continued. "It's because of you that I am now able to see what real love looks like . . . what it feels like. And for that, I love you, Semaj, with everything in me, and I hope that I can be all you need and more."

The smile on his face made my heart swell. He kissed me on the forehead and pulled me into his chest. "What's understood never has to be explained, bae. Only a real man will be willing to do what it takes to keep a smile on his woman's face, and I intend to make you smile for the rest of my life."

Epilogue

One year later . . .

JaNair

It was funny how your life could change over the course of a year. Not only did I graduate with an MBA from Texas A&M University, but I was also now engaged to a man who made it his everyday mission to give me the world.

A lot of shit happened in the months after I returned to California. After ducking and dodging Jerome's calls and pop-up visits for weeks, we finally ran into each other while coming out of the ob-gyn's office one day. Weird place to bump into each other, huh? I thought so, too, seeing as I was there to renew my birth control pills. Jerome, on the other hand, was there to see about the baby girl he and Tangie were having in seven months.

I swear, when Jerome saw my face, it looked like he shit in his pants. I thought it was funny and chuckled a bit. He tried to walk up to me and explain the situation and plead his case about everything that had happened in our relationship, but I stopped him before he could get very far and told him that an explanation wasn't even necessary. I didn't feel any type of way about him getting Tangie pregnant again or even about them together. Like I had told Semaj the night of Tae's party, any ounce of love I had for Jerome had left the minute I found out that not only had he fucked LaLa more than once, but that he had slept with Mya too.

I said my final goodbye to Jerome that day and hadn't seen him since. Tangie and I still talk from time to time, because regardless of the situation, she was a pretty good friend. She did apologize for what happened between her and Jerome, but I forgave her and kept it pushing.

"Baby, what's taking so long?" Semaj yelled from the bottom of the stairs.

I was in our bedroom, packing the last of the luggage we would be taking on our trip to Atlanta, and was running behind. My baby had a few studio sessions with Usher lined up this week, and he was taking me along.

"See, that's why I should leave your ass here. You always gotta pack a suitcase like you're going to be gone for months when it's only going to be for a few days," he said, walking into the room. He smacked me on my ass, then kissed me on my cheek.

"Well, you know I can't really fit into any of my old clothes anymore, so I have to bring a few choices, just in case."

He shook his head at me and laughed. "JaNair, your ass is only a few weeks pregnant. It ain't like you're showing or anything."

Yeah . . . as you can see, that nigga Semaj had hit the bull's-eye and done knocked your girl up. Them damn birth control pills I was on now were no match for that potent-ass sperm his ass was spitting out. Either that or I got pregnant when I switched brands again about a month ago.

"You are glowing, and you look beautiful," Semaj said as he wrapped his arms around my waist and kissed my forehead. "Now, let's go, before I change my mind about introducing you to Usher."

His ass didn't have to tell me twice. I hurried up and zipped up those bags and made my way downstairs. This was our life now. Traveling to different cities and making these hits for all these artists, old and new. Because of the management company I had started, where I managed producers and artists from all different backgrounds, I was able to trek across these states with Semaj whenever our schedules synced up. I was trying to have all the fun I could for the time being because I knew once this baby came, Semaj's ass was going to try to knock me up again.

Semaj

I know JaNair's ass already told y'all the good news, so I'm not going to even repeat it. What I will say, though, is, once she drops my junior, she's going to be giving me my princess before that little nigga even turns one.

Life for your boy couldn't be any better than what it was right now. Since the night of Tae's party in Texas, I'd been getting work left and right. So much so that I was able to purchase the four-bedroom, two-and-a-half bath home we were living in now, pay off my auntie's mortgage and give her the money to start her own catering business, cop Lil Ray a new car and hit him off with some ends for my goddaughter. I also cashed out at Toys "R" Us and started a college fund for Ta'Jae. And speaking of my baby girl, when I got back to California, I almost had to put my foot in Tasha's ass because she was still tripping on bringing my daughter around. One night, after I waited all day for her to bring Ta'Jae to my aunt's house and she never showed up, I hopped in my car and went to her house. When I got there, I banged on the door for about ten minutes before someone finally answered.

"Aye, my nigga, why you knocking on my girl's door like that? You do know what time it is, right?" some Mehcad Brooks–looking muthafucka asked when he came into sight.

"Look, man, I'm sorry for knocking on the door this late, but Tasha gave me no other choice. I've been out of town, working, so I haven't seen my baby in months. For the past few weeks, since I've been back in Cali, I've been asking Tasha to bring my daughter to my aunt's house so that I can spend some time with her. Tasha's dumb ass would have me waiting there all day, only to not show up. Today, though, was the last straw. I'm going to see my baby tonight, and if I have to fight you to get in there and make it happen, then so be it."

Homeboy looked at me for a minute, then over his shoulder. He stepped to the side and told me to come in. I kind of hesitated at first because the shit seemed too easy, but when he stuck his hand out to introduce himself, I figured everything was cool.

"What's up, man? I'm Dre. It's nice to finally meet you."

I shook his hand. "You know who I am?"

He nodded his head. "Yeah. Ta'Jae has your pictures all over her room, and I saw those articles about you in *XXL* and *Vibe*. You doing your thang, fam."

"'Preciate it, man." I looked around the nicely redecorated apartment. There was no doubt that the money from those returned plane tickets had paid for some of this shit. "Where's Tasha and my daughter?"

He sat down on the couch. "Ta'Jae is in her room, asleep, and Tasha went to go grab some condoms." Our eyes connected. "Man, I see the way she does you, and I'm good on having a baby with her . . . on purpose or by accident."

We chopped it up for a few more minutes before I went into my baby's room, packed her an overnight bag, and took her home with me. Tasha used to blow my phone up all day every day when I "kidnapped" my own daughter, but that all had stopped the minute she got that letter from my lawyer in the mail. I was in the process of filing for joint custody of my daughter, because I wanted to be able to have the right to send for my baby and be able to see her when it was my time to have her. The court date was in a couple months, and I had been awarded temporary custody until then.

ShaNiece

Everything in my life was actually going great. I had been promoted to a manager position at my job a few months ago, and I was looking to be promoted again at the end of the quarter. I was happy as hell that I was finally starting to get recognized in my professional life as well as my personal life. My sister and I still weren't on the best of terms, but for the sake of my niece TT's baby, we were cordial around one another. It kind of sucked, though, not having that sisterly bond we used to have.

That was why when Toby proposed to me not too long ago, I wasn't as excited as I should've been. I called my mom and shared the news with her, and of course, she was happy, but not being able to call LaLa or Mya even and enjoy the special moment with my sister and best friend, like most soon-to-be brides did, was fucked up.

"Come in!" I yelled out to whoever was knocking on my new office door.

"Hey, ShaNiece . . . ," my secretary, Lauren, said, peeking her head in the door. "You have a delivery out here."

"Are they the HIPAA releases we've been waiting for from the hospital?"

She shook her head. "I don't think so. This delivery is more on the . . . personal side."

Personal side.

"Okay . . . Well, send it in."

My first thoughts went to Toby, because he'd been surprising me with little gifts ever since we got engaged.

I wouldn't be surprised if this was something he was totally behind.

"Okay. Bring 'em in here," Lauren instructed when she reappeared in my doorway.

Three seconds later, an assembly line of flower arrangements was being placed in every open space in my office. By the time the last bouquet of roses had been brought in, my office looked like a small botanical garden.

"Who are . . . ? What are . . . ?" My office phone rang before I could even form a question. I took the call.

"This is ShaNiece Taylor. How can I assist you?"

"Do you like your surprise?" Toby's deep voice vibrated through the phone.

A smile easily took over my face. "Babe, I love them all, but why so many flowers?"

"Because I want you to see how much I love you."

"I already know how much you love me, Tobias Wright. You tell me that every day."

"Hence the three hundred sixty-five roses I just sent you. Each rose represents a day I've told you that I love you."

My whole body blushed.

"Sometimes I feel like visually showing somebody something is better than just telling them, don't you think?" he added.

I couldn't hold it in anymore and started to cry like a baby. Toby always did shit like this that had me boo-hooing all the time. The last time I had cried this hard was when he slipped the five-carat Tacori platinum diamond engagement ring on my finger.

"Stop all that crying, baby, and get back to work. I'll see later on tonight, when you get home, okay?"

I nodded my head like he could see me.

"I love you, Niecey."

"I love you too, Toby."

I hung up the phone and got back to work, but not before walking over to my wall calendar and crossing out another day.

"Eleven months, three days, and ten hours before I become Mrs. Tobias Wayne Wright, and I can't wait another minute."

Jerome

"Hey, Rome. Can you go to the store and get me some vanilla ice cream and smoked oysters?" Tangie said. "I don't know why I've been craving that weird combination, but I have."

I watched Tangie continue to run her mouth as she walked around the kitchen, trying to get dinner together. Every few steps she'd stop and rub her nine-month belly. The same thing she'd done when she had Lil J.

"Have you talked to Toby today?" she asked.

I shook my head no. She asked me this shit every day, despite knowing I hadn't talked to Toby in a while. We had sorta had this big blowup behind the Lotus Bomb and some missing alcohol and money. Toby and G had felt like I needed to take some time off to get my life together and join an AA group. I, on the other hand, had felt like I didn't need to do shit but drink my life away and wait for JaNair to come back to me. I had been doing well for a while with stealing money from the night's take to feed my alcohol thirst. When Toby had started to ask questions about the missing money and booze, I had easily pointed a finger at some of the new waitresses and waiters, causing them to lose their jobs in the process. About a month later, Toby had called me into his office to show me something he'd seen on the security camera.

"You mind explaining to me what you're doing behind the bar?" he said when I sat down across from him at his desk. He pointed to his computer.

I looked at the screen. Toby and I watched someone who looked like me take liquor from the shelves behind the bar and stuff them into my large duffel bag.

"What are you doing with all that alcohol, bruh? Is that how we're getting down now, Rome? We stealing from ourselves? Getting innocent people fired because you don't want to admit that you have a problem—"

"Look, man—" I began, but he raised his hand, cutting me off.

"Look, man, nothing. Rome, if I can't trust you to keep it real with yourself or me, how can I trust you to run a business? Especially a business that I invested a whole chunk of money in." He blew out a frustrated breath and ran his fingers through his hair. "You know you're my nigga, and we go way back, but until you get some help, I can't continue to do business with you."

He took a white envelope out of a desk drawer and placed in on the desktop. "This is a check for your half of Lotus Bomb, plus interest. As hard as this is for me, I'm buying you out, man. Maybe if you get your shit together in a couple months and still have this money around, we can talk about bringing you back in. Unfortunately, today we're no longer business partners, but hopefully, we're still friends." He extended his hand out to me, but I didn't shake that shit. I stomped out and grabbed all the shit I could from my office and left.

I tried calling JaNair, but I got the automated system, which told me that her number was no longer in service. I went by LaLa's just to talk to her, but she had so much going on with Aspen's real father and fake father that she didn't have time to listen to me. I called G to see if he wanted to go get a few drinks, but he already had plans with Day. After driving around aimlessly for a few hours and drunker than a skunk, I found myself sitting in front of Tangie's house, just looking at her door. It took Lil J coming outside to my car to get me to exit the vehicle. The look on my son's face when I stumbled out of the car, slurring my words and falling all over myself, was enough to make me want to sober up.

After enrolling in an AA class at the hospital Tangie worked at, and after coming to terms with the fact that I was never going to get JaNair back, I started slowly working on getting my life back on track. With the help and love of Tangie and Lil J, I was now nine months sober and looking forward to starting our new family.

LaNiece

"Happy birthday to you. Happy birthday to you. Happy birthday, dear Mommy. Happy birthday to you." Lil Ray and Aspen sang as they sat the homemade confetti cake down in front of me. I looked at the lopsided, horribly decorated creation and couldn't do anything but smile. The execution was all the way off, but the thought was what warmed my heart.

"Go get Mommy's present from our secret hiding spot, Penny, so that she can open it."

"Otay, Daddy," my mini me said as she got up from her spot on Lil Ray's lap. She took off to her bedroom.

Lil Ray shook his head, a smile on his face. "That little girl is something else."

"That she is. But that's my baby."

"You mean *our* baby. That's *our* baby," Lil Ray said, correcting me.

I didn't say anything else, because he was right. Aspen was *our* daughter, and you couldn't tell him any different.

In the past year, Lil Ray had been everything to our daughter that Big Will's dumb ass hadn't or didn't want to be. He was an exclusive member of Aspen's Royal Tea Parties, Nurse Ray when it was time to fix her stuffed animal, Dr. Daddy when she had a boo-boo of her own. Lil Ray was a best friend, first love, and so much more to that little girl.

"Has her donor called today?" I heard Ray ask as he cut pieces of the cake and placed them at our spots on the table.

"He hasn't called at all. I'ma give him a couple more hours. If nothing, then"—I shrugged my shoulders—"oh well." This was supposed to be the weekend Will picked Aspen up, in keeping with the court order from our custody hearing, but he never stuck to it. I was pretty sure he knew today was my and Niecey's birthday, so him not showing up was his way of fucking up my plans.

"If he doesn't come to pick her up, just call you mom or Niecey and see if one of them can watch her."

I shook my head. "You already know Toby got something elaborate planned for Niecey, so she's out of the question, and Mom is still on that cruise with her little boyfriend of hers."

"Let me find out you hating on Ms. Pam." Lil Ray laughed.

"Boy, please. That nigga she dating is young enough to be my son."

We both laughed.

"You know I like my meat a little more tender than that," I added. "That good old corn-fed beef. That nice and juicy Grade A USDA beef."

"Oh yeah?" He licked his lips, and I nodded my head. "I better be the only beef you like," he said before he leaned over the table and kissed my lips.

"Daddy kiss Mommy . . . Daddy kiss Mommy . . . Do it again, Daddy. Do it again . . ." Aspen stood at the edge of the table, with the biggest smile on her face, clapping her hands and waiting for her daddy to fulfill her request. This little girl loved to see Lil Ray and me kiss.

I pulled one of her pigtails on top of her head and was rewarded with a frown.

"You don't like Mommy touching your hair?" I asked her.

She stubbornly shook her head and walked over to her daddy.

"Oh, it's like that, huh? Okay . . . I'ma remember that when you want Mommy to read you that princess book you love so much," I told her.

The heffa actually looked up at me and rolled her eyes before she sat back on her daddy's lap. I picked up the little gift she had left on the floor, removed the card from the top, and opened it.

"Aw . . . thank you, stink. You got Mommy her favorite Disney movie, *Pocahontas*. Come give me a hug." Aspen hopped off Ray's lap and ran into my open arms.

"Can we watch *Hun-tuss*, Mommy, please?"

I looked at Lil Ray, who nodded his head, silently giving me a rain check on my birthday date. "Okay, baby. Let Mommy read your card first, and then we can go, okay?"

She nodded her head, then snatched the movie out of my hands and gave it to her daddy to open.

This little girl was going to be the death of me. I flipped the pink envelope over and tore open the sealed flap. I pulled out the card, expecting to see some type of cartoon character depicted on the front, something Aspen would choose, and was surprised when I saw two glasses of wine, a piece of cake on a plate, and a few party decorations on a table instead. I opened the card up and automatically recognized the person's handwriting.

LaLa,
We're not at a place right now where I'm ready to kick it like we used to, but that doesn't mean I can't send you some warm birthday wishes. I hope you have a wonderful day today and get everything you've ever wished for. Tell my friend Penny I said hi and that I'll see that alligator later.
Happy birthday again . . .
~J

This was the second-best gift I could have received today. Not only was I going to spend my day with my two most favorite people in the world, but JaNair had finally reached out to me after so many failed attempts on my part. I couldn't wait until the day that we were back hanging around each other. I really missed my friend.

Mya

Well, it's finally my turn to catch you guys up on what's been going on in my life. As hard as it may be to believe, I'm actually doing okay.

The slashes on my face finally healed. Nonetheless, the Z-shaped scar on the left side of my face and the V-shaped scar on the right side were going to be permanent reminders of what happened. You would think that I'd be upset with the way I looked now, because my looks were what used to get me everything I wanted, but honestly, I could actually sit here and say that I was not upset at all. Yeah, the scars caused a lot of people to stare, but the fact that I was still alive and able to see them staring at me with both of my eyes had me feeling a different type of way.

After I'd been discharged from the hospital, I'd packed up everything I had left inside JaNair's old house and moved all the way to Florida, to stay with my aunt and uncle. I missed living in Cali, but it had been more than time for me to leave. Being in a different state was something I really had to get adjusted to, but I was handling it quite well. I had found a job at a local boutique. Had got me a new car about three months ago, and was finally moving into my own place this weekend.

So, like I said earlier, I was actually doing okay. The only thing missing now was a man to spend a little time with. I wasn't trying to rush into anything too soon or anything like that, but I was open to going out on dates and doing things of that nature. There was only one main requirement that I needed him to fulfill, and that was to have a relationship status of completely single.

The End

Also by genesis woods

Diamond Mafia:

How a Good Girl Set It Off

Prologue

"Yo, you really think all four of them broads gon' be down with your plan?"

I sat back in my seat and eyed the small group of people who stood around a huge birthday cake, singing the age-old song to a little boy decked out in Gucci from head to toe. His wide eyes wandered around in amazement at all the people who circled him with smiles on their faces as they sang off-key. A little girl I was assuming to be his sister stood next to him. Her hair was layered in French braids with colorful beads at the end, and she wore an outfit similar to his, but hers was pink. You could tell by the little pout on her cute face that she was feeling some type of way about not getting all the attention, but she quickly got over it when her brother stepped to the side and allowed her to blow out each of the burning candles on top of his cake. The four women I was interested in proposing this job to all cheered the little girl on as she started to dance shortly after, tongues and phones all out while they snapped pictures and moved to the beat as well.

Wiping my hand over my face, I silently counted to five and sighed. This was why I liked to research potential workers on my own. Niggas like Ant could work your last nerve, always wanting to know the if, ands, buts, or whys behind certain shit happening. The only reason I kept him around was because he was family, and the nigga was actually good at what he did.

"I think anybody would be down with making some money. Especially when there's *eighty million* reasons why they should," I expressed, putting emphasis on the amount of money we stood to make if everything went according to plan.

Ant looked back over toward the crowd of people, who were now all dancing and eating cake as the sounds of Ice Cube's classic song "Today Was a Good Day" rattled loudly from the trunk of a '64 Impala.

"You think I can crack one of these hoes before you get them to come on board?" He chucked his chin up. "The one with the short haircut is who I'm feeling. She got a thick little frame and is bad as fuck."

My eyes wandered over to the girl he was talking about. She was a sexy little piece, around five-seven, with smooth milk chocolate skin; eyes almond-shaped and bright like the sun; lips full, ass fat, waist small, and titties just right. I felt a sudden pull in my groin as my gaze continued to scan her thick frame from head to toe. As if she could feel my intense glare on her, she paused putting the hunk of cake in her mouth and looked around the park at her surroundings. For a split second, her eyes cut to where I was parked, but then changed direction when she couldn't see behind the dark tint on my windows.

"That one"—I pointed in her path—"is off limits."

"Off limits? But—"

I cut him off. "But nothing. That girl right there is the key to my plan actually going through. I'm not about to let you fuck up anything for me or the rest of the crew."

Ant sucked his teeth. "Nigga, you ain't slick one bit. Talking about *she's the key to my plan going through,*" he said, poorly mocking my deep voice. "I know you, my dude, and I can tell from the look in your eyes that you want her all for yourself. That's why she's really off limits. Tell the truth and shame the devil, my nigga. Since when have you ever had a problem with me mixing business with pleasure? You know how many hoes I done fucked that have worked for you and you ain't said not one single word? As long as they—"

"Get to the money." We finished the last of his sentence together and laughed.

"I'm saying, though." Ant raised his hands, still chuckling. "Shawty look like she can be the next Mrs. Lewis if I'm keeping it all the way real. I'd wife her ass up in a second."

I looked back over at the crowd of people who were still partying and having a good time. The woman who'd had my attention since the first time I laid eyes on her a couple days ago was talking to a redbone chick who had just walked up to the little get-together. I watched as she smiled that beautiful smile of hers and hugged the girl tightly around her neck. She took the gift bag from the girl's hand and placed it on the table before pulling her over to the tree where the other three women she rolled with were standing.

"Aye, pass me that folder out of the glove compartment," I advised Ant as I looked at a text on my phone, ignoring his last comment. Once he handed it over to me, I opened it up and passed him three of the four pictures that were paper-clipped to the top. "I need you to study each and every one of their faces. In the next few weeks, I want you to find out everything there is to know about each of them—where they work, what type of car they drive, the brand of maxi pads they wear when it's that time of the month. I wanna know who they're related to, who they're associated with, and who they're fucking even if it's off and on. I need to know everything."

Ant nodded as he shuffled through the photos. "I got you, man. But, uh, what about that picture over there, though? The one you got that tight grip on." I looked down at the photo of the chocolate beauty I held in my hand and then over to the tree where she was still standing. Snoop Dogg's "3's Company" was blasting through the speakers as the little birthday boy did his rendition of a crip walk with the woman I was assuming to be his mother c-walking right along with him.

"Don't worry about her. I'm going to personally look into her background," I said, grabbing at the fine hairs on my chin. "Like I said, she's the most important piece to this puzzle, and I'm not about to let you fuck that up."

Ant cut his eyes at me before grabbing the folder out of my lap and looking over the paperwork inside.

"So, other than this bullshit your tech guy was able to get off the internet, have you heard anything from them niggas you keep on payroll in the hood about these broads?"

I thought about his question for a second. "I haven't heard anything of importance yet. However, this one right here—" I grabbed the picture of the Keri Hilson lookalike. "Her nigga is someone we both have crossed paths with before."

Ant squinted his eyes at the photo, trying to see if he could place her face somewhere. He shook his head. "She doesn't look familiar at all. Who's her nigga?"

My lips curled into a slick grin. "Remember that muthafucka Big Titty Tina brought to your welcome home party a few months back?"

He nodded his head slowly.

"Found out she"—I pointed at the picture—"is his old lady."

He covered his mouth with his fist. "Noooooooooo. I know he ain't fucking around on her fine ass with Tina big ass?"

I shook my head and laughed. "Aye, don't do my homie Tina like that. You know she be pulling these dummies left and right. Be getting paid, too."

"I'm saying, though," Ant said, still amazed. His eyes zeroed in on the picture of the girl with caramel skin, honey-colored eyes, and long blonde hair. "Tina pussy and head gotta be hella fiyah if this nigga is fucking around on his fine-ass girl with her. Maaaaaan . . . I'm at a loss for words." He shook his head. "I don't even wanna talk about this shit anymore. Did you roll up on Tina yet?"

I nodded my head. "You know I did. Dropped a few bands on her too."

Ant sat up in his seat and rubbed his hands together, excitement all over his face. "Okay. And what did her *do-anything-for-money* ass tell you?"

"She didn't tell me much because she said the nigga is real secretive about his shit. However,"—I licked my lips—"she did tell me a little something that I think will get you started in the right direction when looking into ole girl."

He nodded his head as he turned his eyes back toward the party, which was still going on. "Well, what are you waiting for, nigga? Lay it on me."

I looked down at the picture in my hand and smiled. My dick was getting harder and harder each time I thought about the money we were about to make and the pretty face I intended to have in my bed before this was all over with. After zoning out for a second, I turned my attention back to Ant and said, "All right then, so check it . . ."

Chapter 1

Lucinda "Lucci" Adams

I get high, high, high (Every day)
I get high, high, high (Every night)
I get high, high, high (All the time)
High.

Styles P's classic "Good Times" knocked through my speakers as I sped down the 105 freeway, finally making my way back to the city from a twelve-hour turn-around trip I just did to Arizona. I'd been up for the last twenty-four hours doing what I did best, making that money. Now, normally I wouldn't make a run like this because my man Stax and I had a whole army of workers under us who got paid to do it, but when the money started to come up short and product started to slowly disappear, that's when one of us had to show face and get shit back on track. Since Stax was taking care of a different situation, it was my turn to make this trip.

Hopping off of my exit on Wilmington Avenue, I maneuvered my way through the back streets of ghetto-ass Watts until I arrived at the tiny stash house we had tucked deep in the heart of this small city. Fiends were walking around, looking for their next hit, while niggas who thought they were making money stood on the corner, clocking hours that we allowed them to get.

Young girls pranced around in this summer heat wearing short-ass Daisy Dukes and crop tops, looking for the next baller to take them up out the hood.

I smirked and shook my head as I passed by my girl Kay Kay's little sister, Shauna, and the pack of rats she always kept behind her. The girl was always on this side of town, trying to get picked, but never got with a nigga worth anything. She already had two kids at home that she cared nothing about, but she was still out here busting it open for whoever was willing to pay like they weighed.

I pulled into the driveway of the trap house we mainly used to cook and bag our dope, happy to see Stax was already there waiting on me.

"What's up, Lucci?" Zig, one of our enforcers, yelled out as soon as my feet hit the ground.

I grabbed the black duffle bags out of the back seat of my truck and closed the door.

"What's up, Zig? Where it's at?"

He held his hands up in the air and smiled, pausing the dice game he and some of the other workers were in the middle of.

"Shit, you know I stay with that good green. You matching one or what?"

I chucked my chin up toward the house. "Let me go take care of this first, and then we can roll a couple up."

His thick lips curled into a sexy-ass smile before he nodded his head. "All right, bet. I'ma be out here when you get done in there with boss man. I need to holla at you about something too." A more serious look took over his boyishly handsome features. "Something went down at Tuni's spot on Sixth Ave last night, and shit ain't adding up."

I stopped in my tracks at the news and walked over toward Zig, who stepped away from his dice game and met me halfway. The YSL cologne he had on met me before he did. My eyes roamed over his six-foot-two frame and decadent chocolate skin. His signature low taper cut was looking like he'd just stepped fresh out of the barber's chair; thick gold link chain hanging from his neck with the matching bracelet around his wrist. A simple black T-shirt with the words *#MoneyMoves* across his chest and black 501 jeans was his outfit of choice, topped off with some tight-ass red sneakers that I knew probably cost a grip and a red bandana hanging out of his back pocket on the right. Even in the neighborhood we were in, Zig stayed reppin' his colors, and I liked that about him. I liked that a lot.

Biting down on my lip, I tried to suppress the low moan that escaped my mouth when he walked up on me, hovering over my body. The look in his eyes was one I couldn't describe as he eyed me up and down as well. I cleared my throat and stepped back a little when I started to feel curious eyes looking in our direction. Everyone knew I was Stax's girl and would lie, die, steal, and kill for that nigga. However, it didn't stop me from being attracted to this fine man standing in front of me.

"So, what happened on Sixth Ave?" I asked in a voice I didn't even recognize.

Zig smirked after realizing the effect he had on me. Instead of speaking on the situation at hand, he chuckled and said, "When you gon' stop fucking with that nigga Stax and come get up with a real nigga?"

"A real nigga?" I questioned, mind already going back into the trance Zig's fine ass had me in.

"Yeah, a real nigga. If you were my girl, you wouldn't be out here making the type of moves that you be making. Nah." He rubbed his hands together and licked his lips. "You would be out shopping with your girls, getting your hair done, and all that girly shit females like to do."

I cocked my head to the side, eyes in a low squint, as his words replayed in my mind. "It's obvious you don't know me that well. I've always been a get-money bitch and always will be. My man would know and understand that I don't like to just sit in the house and spend up all his money. It's a must that I have my own, and the only way to do that is to get out here and get it how I live." I walked up closer to him and could see the pure look of lust in his eyes, "So see, my dear Zig, you and I could never be. You want a good girl or one of those bird bitches"—my head nodded in the direction of Shauna and her friends walking down the street—"like them hoes, and I'm far from that."

Zig opened his mouth to say something but stopped when the dice game he had just left started to get a little too heated. Before he could even turn back around to address me, I was already walking off and headed back toward the rear of the house. I shook my head and laughed.

Zig and I grew up in the same projects, the Nickerson Gardens. We were cool and hung out a time or two, but nothing ever really happened between us. By the time I started taking niggas serious and really fucking around with them, Stax had entered my life and shut down all of the situationships I had going on outside of him. I was a thug-ass bitch who needed a thug-ass nigga. Zig was still working his way up, and Stax was already out there making moves, so the choice was easy for me to make. I just hoped that my decision to sleep next to a nigga who was as money hungry and cutthroat as me would never blow up in my face.

"What's up, Lucci?"

"Hey, Lucci."

Females greeted me after I stepped into the one-story rundown house and into the kitchen. Bitches Stax had on the payroll were asshole naked, cutting and bagging up our dope.

"What's up, Cyn and Moni?" I returned. They were the only chicks who talked to me out of the six that were there, and for good reason. Cyn and Moni were the only two hoes I didn't have to pistol whip for stepping out of line and trying to get at Stax behind my back. Since the beatdown of the last girl I fired, I hadn't had any real problems out of anyone. These bitches knew I was crazy and wouldn't hesitate to kill the fuck out of one of them if they tried that shit again.

Walking down the hallway, I passed up the two rooms Stax usually used to test out the dope with a few fiends and the main bathroom everyone had to use. Once I made it to the double doors at the end of the hallway, I knocked on the door a few times before opening it and walking in. Stax was sitting behind his desk, reading something on his phone and smiling hard as fuck. He was so into whoever he was texting that he didn't notice I was there until I dropped the money-filled duffle bags on the ground, causing a loud thump to echo around us.

"What's up, baby?" he finally said when his eyes landed on me. The phone in his hand was placed on his desk face down. "When did you get here?"

"Who got your ass smiling like that?" I asked, ignoring his greeting and question.

"Man Lucci, don't start that shit. You just got back. A nigga can't get a hug or a kiss?"

"Not until you tell me who the fuck has you skinning and grinning the way you just were when I walked in," I said as I walked closer to his desk. I reached my hand out to grab his phone, but he snatched it before I could get it.

"Lucci, you know better than that. Since when do we start checking each other's phones and shit? You know what type of thangs go on around here, so you know anything that happens on this phone"—he held up the blue-cased iPhone—"is strictly business. Now, if I were on the personal line, I could see you questioning me about some shit, but this phone, you know its business only."

I stared at Stax for a few seconds, knowing his Henry Simmons–looking ass wasn't telling me the whole truth, but I decided to let it go for now. I hadn't seen my man in the last twenty-four hours, and all I wanted to do was count this money and get some dick.

Stax placed his phone back on the desk and stood up. With his arms opened wide, he walked up to me and pulled me into his embrace. His cologne didn't have me stuck like Zig's did a few minutes ago, but it was familiar and welcoming, something I needed right now.

"How did everything go?" Stax finally asked as we pulled apart. He kissed my forehead and then grabbed my hand, pulling me over to his seat, where he sat back down and placed my ass directly on his dick. "Them niggas didn't disrespect you or come at you wrong, did they?"

I waved him off. "Everything went cool. Dayo tried to run game on me, but I nipped that shit in the bud as soon as his lying ass started the bullshit up. I had to whip my piece out on his right hand, too, because the nigga thought that just because I was a woman, our meeting was gon' go a certain way."

"Niggas ain't knowing about my down-ass bitch Lucci. Did you get the money he owed us?"

"Nigga, do you know who you talking to? Them niggas knew what was up as soon as I kicked in the door and walked in that muthafucka. Had to slap the little bitch sucking Dayo's dick. She wouldn't stop screaming. But once I pointed that gun at her ass, she shut right the fuck up."

Stax chuckled and slapped me on my ass, garnering a surprised yelp out of me.

"Stop, babe. My shit already hurting from sitting in that car so long."

"You want me to rub it for you?" he asked, placing his big hands on my thighs and massaging them.

I moaned. "I want you to do more than rub my thighs, baby. Your pussy needs some loving too."

"Is that right?" A slow smirk formed on his face as I stood up from his lap and began to undress. His eyes stayed on me the whole time until I was completely naked. He licked his lips when he looked down at my hairless mound. "You know I missed my pussy, right? Nigga couldn't even think straight without her around."

"Showing is always better than telling."

Before I knew it, Stax picked me up and laid me on his big oak desk, knocking all of his papers and shit onto the floor. My legs, which were already in the air, were pushed open and spread far apart before I felt the tip of his tongue playing with my clit. My back arched the second he pulled my pearl into his mouth and sucked on it so hard that I exploded all over his face.

Although I was enjoying the way Stax dined on what truly belonged to him, I couldn't shake the visions of Zig being down there instead. I would never betray Stax for no other nigga, because he would never do me that way; however, imagining Zig's thick, juicy lips sucking on my shit had me busting harder than I ever had before.

Chapter 2

Diamond Morris

"Hey, Diamond, once you're done with that customer, can you come to my office for a second?"

I internally groaned and tried hard as fuck not to roll my eyes at my assistant manager, who liked to micromanage the fuck out of me. Ever since corporate gave pimply-face Timmy his promotion, his ass had really been on one.

After bagging the customer's food and giving her change, I closed out my register and walked to the back of the store to Timmy's closet-sized office. Not even bothering to knock on the door, I entered his shit and instantly turned my nose up. The pungent smell of ass and some sort of medicated cream hit my nostrils as soon as I stepped in.

"You wanted to see me, Tim?" I asked in a not-so-enthused voice.

He typed something on his computer, fingers hitting the keys hard as hell before pushing his glasses up the bridge of his nose and looking up at me.

"Have a seat, Diamond."

I shook my head. "Nah, I rather stand."

He shrugged his shoulders and pushed his glasses up again. "Okay, well, I'm looking over your timecard for the last week, and I noticed that you've been clocking in late every day except for today. Care to explain the reasons behind your tardiness, Ms. Morris?"

I thought for a second before I opened my mouth. If I told him the real reason behind me being late, he would probably question my ability to perform my job and whether I could still work there with having so much on my plate. On the other hand, I didn't want to lie to him. I mean, I did have a legitimate reason behind me being late in the last few days. Well, I should say weeks, if I was being completely honest.

I removed the pinwheel hat from my head and walked farther into his office. After looking around at the pictures of his ugly-ass family on the wall and the mountain of paperwork scattered around, I took a deep breath and gave him my explanation.

"Well Tim, I've been late this last week because I've been at the hospital—"

"You were in the hospital?" he asked, cutting me off.

"No. I've been *at* the hospital. You see, my twin brother had a massive heart attack a month ago, and I'm the only family he has. So, I go to see him and talk to his doctors about his progress in the morning, and then I ride the train here. After I clock out from Hot Dog on a Stick, I go straight to my second job at the department store downstairs. I work there until closing, and then I go to my third job I have at this small bar on the other side of town. Sometimes I don't make it home until three in the morning if the buses are running slow. I get home, sleep for about four hours, and then start the day all over again."

Tim looked at something on his computer screen and then back up at me. "So, you are working three jobs right now? Is there a reason why you need to work all three? Maybe if you quit one, things will be a little easier on you. Probably get to see your brother more and get a little more sleep."

"I need to work three jobs. It's the only way I can afford to pay my bills and my brother's hospital bills. His insurance only pays so much, and the rest has to come out of my pocket. And then the doctors are saying he has some brain damage, so when he does get better, he will have to have a nurse caring for him around the clock once he's discharged."

My eyes began to water as thoughts of my brother lying in his hospital bed flashed through my mind. Who would have ever thought that at thirty-one, someone as healthy as he was could have a heart attack? I didn't believe it when I got the call that he had collapsed while playing a game of basketball at the gym with his friends. I wasn't prepared for the tubes sticking out of his mouth and nose when I walked into his hospital room. Nor was I prepared to see him lying stiff with no signs of life in his body, either. The machine he was hooked up to was breathing for him now. In a couple of days, the doctors were going to slowly take it off of him to see if he could breathe on his own. I was praying like crazy that he came out of this. I needed my brother back. I needed his smile, his laugh, his love. I needed my everything.

"Wow, Diamond, I'm sorry to hear about your brother and everything you're going through."

"Thanks, Tim," I replied, wiping a lone tear from my eye.

He nodded his head. "Do you think that maybe you should be moved to a later shift instead of opening? That way you have enough time to handle your business in the morning."

I opened my mouth on the verge of saying something smart, but closed it when I felt my attitude start to spike up. Instead of saying what I wanted to say to this dork-ass muthafucka, I took a deep breath and responded in a less aggressive way.

"That wouldn't work for me because of my other jobs. If I started later here, that would throw my whole schedule off and make me late for those."

His eyebrow arched. "So, you're on time at your other jobs?"

"Not all the time, but for the most part, yes. My other supervisors understand and know the hardship I'm going through right now, so they don't really trip off of me coming in a few minutes late."

He scoffed. "You call thirty, sometimes forty-five minutes *a few minutes late*?" He used air quotes to mock me.

"No, but I can only get here as fast as the bus allows me to."

Tim shook his head before looking over at me with sympathetic eyes. "Look, Diamond, I feel for you and what you're going through. However, your tardiness is a concern to me. And now that I'm looking over your timesheets for the last month, this isn't the first time you've been late a whole week." Tim took a breath. "I hate to do this to you, but I'm going to have to place you on temporary suspension until myself and the higher-ups can come to a decision as to whether or not you're fit to stay working for the company. Right now, you're more of a liability than an asset. With all that you have going on and not having any reliable transportation, I don't know if you should continue working for—"

"Are you fucking serious?" I yelled, interrupting him, not giving a fuck about how aggressive my tone was now. "At Hot Dog on a Stick? Muthafucka, you act like this is a Fortune 500 company or something where they make real money. Nigga, you probably pull in two *G*s at the most on a good day. I'm the best goddamn employee you have. And now you wanna fire me?"

He raised his hands, palms stretched out to me. "Whoa. Whoa. No one said anything about firing. I said temporary suspension."

"Until you and the higher-ups can decide if I'm fit to stay here or not, right?"

Tim opened and closed his mouth a few times before speaking again. "Diamond, I'm just doing what—"

I held my hand up to stop him from speaking. "You know what? Save that shit. Save it before I put my foot so far up your ass that I can scratch your tonsil with my toenails." The look on Tim's face after I said that would've been funny had I not been so mad. "And you can save your little funky temporary suspension speech, because I quit."

He sprang up from his desk. "Now, wait a minute, Diamond. You don't have to quit."

"I'm supposed to just wait until you fire me then, right?" I shook my head and turned to walk toward the door. "You know, the only reason why I took this job was to help pay some bills. I'm thirty-one years old. I shouldn't even be working at no damn corn dog spot."

Tim mumbled something.

"What did you say?"

He licked his lips nervously. "I said we don't serve corn dogs. We serve *hot dogs* on a stick."

My eyebrows furrowed, and I could feel a nasty curl form on my lip. "Muthafucka, those things are corn dogs, just like that cheap cheese you dip in batter is a fancy mozzarella stick. Fuck outta here. I'll be expecting my last paycheck sometime tomorrow. Don't bother trying to send it in the mail either. I'll be here first thing in the morning to pick it up," I said over my shoulder as I walked out of his office and back to the front.

Grabbing a bag, I dumped in the freshly made corn dogs and cheese sticks my coworker had made for the long line of customers waiting on their orders. I filled my thermos with some of the pink lemonade, said my *fuck-you-see-you-laters,* and then left.

The sound of Tim screaming my name and the waiting customers' complaints were the last things I heard as I stepped on the escalator and made my way down to Macy's. Hopefully my manager there would let me clock in a few hours early to make up for the hours I was going to miss at Hot Dog on a Stick. What started out as a good day for me was easily turning into one of the worst days of my life, especially after I got the call that my brother had another mini heart attack, causing me to leave Macy's early and call out of my nighttime gig.

As I sat on the train on my way to St. Mary's Medical Center, I said a small prayer. "God, please make a way for me to come up on enough money so that I'm able to quit these jobs and take care of my brother without stressing. You know how bad I need Shine to come back to me. He's all I got, and I need him here. Please just let something work in my favor this one time, and I promise I won't ask you for anything else again. Amen."

I didn't know what was in store for me as far as getting more money, but I would gladly do whatever it took to get it. I just hoped it wasn't something that would land me in jail for the rest of my life or get me killed. However, knowing my luck, I'd probably end up working four more part-time jobs at the mall before some fast money shit like that ever happened.

Chapter 3

Robette "Bobbi" Smith

I was wiping down the display cases in the front of the store when the door buzzed, alerting me that security was allowing someone to come in. Placing the towel behind the counter, I smoothed the front of my black blazer down and put a bright smile on my face.

"Welcome to Bernfeld Jewelry Exchange, where diamonds are everyone's best friend. My name is Robette, and I will be your jewelry consultant today. How may I help you?"

My breath caught the second my eyes connected with the same man who had been coming into the store at least twice a week for the last month. He went under security and the owner's radar because he always bought something whenever he came in, but my hood instincts recognized a jack boy when I saw one. His fine ass had been casing the place and I knew it, but his secret was safe with me.

"So, we meet again, Robette," his smooth voice sang once he finally made it over to me.

I took in the three-piece Italian suit tailored only for his body. His chiseled chin and strong jawline was covered with thick, silky hairs. His tall, medium-built frame was a sight to see and probably grabbed the attention of girls everywhere he went. My eyes scanned over the fancy Rolex on his wrist and the sapphire-and-diamond cufflinks he purchased last week on the ends of his shirt. The brother screamed money in every way that you could imagine, but I could tell from the jailhouse tats on his neck and fingers that he was far from it. Nigga was probably born and raised in South Central like me but getting his money the best way he knew how—stealing it.

"Yeah, we do meet again, Mr. . . ." I trailed off, forgetting his name.

"Ali, but please, call me Naveen or Nav. Whichever you prefer." He grabbed my hand to shake, and just like last time, an electric shot zapped through my body.

"Mr.—" I cleared my throat. "I mean Nav, it's nice to see you again. Were . . . were you looking for anything in particular this week? Perhaps some diamond earrings for your mother or girlfriend this time?"

Nav smiled and bit his lip, eyes roaming over the display of diamond earrings in front of me. From studs to hoops to the fancy shit some of the stars wore on the red carpet, we had it all.

"That's a clever way to see if I'm single or not."

I smiled, and he returned it.

"I am a happily married man."

He raised his hand, and I noticed the platinum band around his ring finger for the first time. I tried to hide the shocked look on my face by turning my head to the side and pretending to cough, but I knew he had seen it by the playful gleam in his eye.

"Don't be embarrassed. You couldn't have known. I just recently got married. The weekend before last. That's why I've been in here so much. Had to buy a few gifts and things before the big day."

I slowly nodded my head and began to remove the diamonds from the display case so that he could get a better look.

"Well, um, congratulations on your nuptials, and I wish you many years of wedded bliss."

"Thank you, Robette. Now, if you were my wife, which pair of earrings would you like?"

For the next hour and a half, I assisted Nav with finding a post-wedding gift for his new bride that would be sure to have her gushing for days. After dropping a whopping ten grand on some bomb-ass studded hoops, a two-karat stunning tennis bracelet, and this beautiful emerald teardrop necklace that I would literally kill for, Nav finally left the store and left me to tend to the rest of the customers who were coming in to purchase our jewels.

By the time seven o'clock rolled around, I was tired as shit from selling, showing, inspecting, and cleaning diamonds. I was ready to pack up and take my ass home. On the way to the back room to grab my things, I answered my ringing phone.

"What's up, Diamond? Everything good?"

The quietness on the other end of the line told me that it wasn't.

"I . . . I almost lost him today," Diamond said just above a whisper. "But the doctors were able to keep him alive for the time being."

I already knew she was talking about her brother. He'd been in the hospital for some time now after that heart attack. My girl was stretching herself thin as hell working all those jobs to keep up with bills and shit. I'd offered her money, and so had Lucci and Kay Kay, but Diamond's stubborn ass wouldn't take it. She declined our offers so much that Lucci went behind her back and paid some of the mounting bills adding up. I was pretty sure the hospital informed Diamond about the payments, but she hadn't said anything yet.

"What happened, baby? What's going on?"

As Diamond explained everything going on with Shine, I text both Lucci and Kay Kay, telling them that we needed to head over to the hospital and give our girl some support. Once they both responded with okays, I continued to listen to Diamond and gather all my personal belongings so that I could leave.

"I just don't know what I'm going to do, Bobbi. Not only did I quit one of my jobs that I really needed, but the doctors want my permission to move Shine to some other hospital that's better equipped to keep him alive. The thing is, the transport is going to be risky as hell. They're saying he could die while being airlifted to another hospital." The line went quiet for a few seconds. "I can't lose my brother, Bobbi. I can't lose Shine."

"Shhhhhhh." I tried calming her down. "Everything will be okay, girl. Look, Lucci, Kay Kay, and I are on our way up there. Don't make any decisions until we are all there with you. I'm in line about to get scanned by the security guards, and then I'll call you once I make it to the car, okay?"

"Okay," she sniffled. "I won't make any decisions. Can you . . . can you just try to hurry up? I know traffic is going to be a mess for you all the way out there in Beverly Hills, but please get here as soon as you can."

"I will," I promised her as I walked up to the security guard desk and placed my things on the conveyor belt. "Look, Diamond, I'm about to get checked. Let me call you back."

She giggled. "I can't believe they check you guys like they're the TSA or something. It's gotta be hard as hell to steal diamonds out of a jewelry store. All those cameras they have on you guys every second of the day and security precautions. It's like Fort Knox up in there."

"Shit, it might as well be with all of the diamonds that come through here. I remember one time, we had to shut down because one of the actresses going to the Oscars had a necklace made with over five million dollars of yellow di—Wait. Diamond, let me call you back."

I released the call before she could say anything. After getting my body scanned with the wand, I walked over to the security desk where my things were being held, thumb wavering over Diamond's name so that I could call her back.

"Um, I'm sorry. Why are you guys holding my bag and coat hostage like that?" I asked one of the security guards when I noticed my belongings weren't on the conveyor belt anymore.

He cleared his throat after whispering something to his partner. "Uh, Ms. Smith, Mr. Bernfeld would like to see you in his office."

I looked around the room, staring back at my other coworkers, who were nosily looking over at me. "In his office?" I asked as I turned back around to face him. "Why?"

The security guard cleared his throat again. "Seems like you had something in your personal belongings that didn't belong, and he would like to have a word with you."

"Something in my bag?" I was confused. I'd never stolen anything, or tried to steal anything for that matter, so what the hell were they talking about? I reached my hand out over the desk. "Please give me my things. Let me see what you're talking about."

"Unfortunately, I can't give you your stuff at this time, Ms. Smith." He pulled my bag further out of my reach.

"Why not?"

"Because of the evidence."

"Evidence!" I screamed loudly this time. "What the fuck are you talking about, evidence? I ain't steal shit."

"Ms. Smith," he hissed, trying to control the situation.

"Ms. Smith my ass. Give me my bag. Show me what the fuck you found as evidence. I'm not about to leave my shit up here so you can plant something in it. Y'all got me all the way fucked up if you think I'm going to let that go down. Muthafuckas, I'm from the hood, the product of a street rat and a scammer, so you gon' have to come with something pretty wild to get one over on me."

"Ms. Smith"

"Nah, fuck that," I started, but stopped when the stern voice of Mr. Josh Bernfeld, part owner of Bernfeld

Jewelry Exchange, called my name. I turned around in his direction with wild eyes, wondering what the hell was going on.

"Ms. Smith, if you just come to my office, we can talk about everything privately."

"Privately? I feel like I'm being treated like a criminal for something I know I didn't do."

He walked closer to where I was standing, hands up in surrender, eyes focused on my face, voice low and calming. He reminded me of those negotiators on the TV shows that try to talk down a hostage situation.

"Robette, please. If you would just follow me to my office, I promise that we will get everything under control and figure this out."

After thinking about it for a few seconds, I said, "I'll come, but I'm not leaving my bag up here for them to plant some shit in it."

Mr. Bernfeld walked over to the desk and grabbed my things. "Can we go now?"

I nodded my head and turned toward the direction of his office. A million things were going through my mind as we walked down the long hallway, my heels click-clacking on the linoleum floor. The line of fluorescent lights above me got brighter the closer we got to our destination. I stopped just as we reached the cherrywood door with the gold plaque on it that read JOSHUA BERN-FELD in big black letters.

Stepping to the side, I watched as he slipped his key into the knob and pushed the heavy piece open. Walking in first, I looked around the poshly decorated office with its grey, red, and black color scheme. It had been a hot minute since I'd been in there. The sound of the door shutting closed brought me back from my thoughts.

Just as I opened my mouth to ask what this really was about, my back was slammed against the door, and my blazer and shirt were ripped open.

"God, I couldn't wait to get you back here," Josh breathed into my ear as his hands fondled my breasts. "I've been watching you on the security camera all day. I saw you flirting with that tattooed thug, too. Is he your type, Robette? Huh? You think he can fuck you better than I can?"

"No," I breathlessly lied as he took one of my nipples in his mouth and sucked hard on it. "He's . . . he's married any . . . anyway."

"What does that mean?" he managed to ask with a mouth full of titty.

"It means—*oh*. It means I don't . . . fuck with . . . with married men." I could hardly get a word out. Josh had his hand on my nub, thumping it with his fingers. I was on the verge of cumming and was getting tongue tied in the process.

"I'm sorry I made such a big spectacle to get you back here," he apologized in between breaths. "But I didn't know any other way I could get you into my office without people questioning me having you back here for no reason."

So that's what all this was about. Although I was mad as fuck from being embarrassed in front of all those people, I didn't have the desire to address that right now. All I wanted was some dick before I left to go to the hospital. This was going to be the last time Josh and I had sex, and I really meant it this time.

What had started out as a little harmless flirting when I needed a few extra hours some months ago had easily turned into this three-month affair Josh and I now had going on. He was not typically my type. I'd never ever seen myself actually fucking him, but when my curiosity got the best of me after staying late to help with inventory one evening, Josh surprised me with his stroke game, and we'd been fucking ever since.

"Damn, I can't wait to put your pussy in my face and taste it."

"Me either. You got protection, right? You know if there's no glove, there's—"

"No love," he finished for me. "Yes, I have condoms. Bought a whole new pack on my lunch break."

I smirked at his audacity. "Okay, but we are going to have to make this quick. I gotta meet my friends at the hospital, and I don't wanna be the last one holding them up."

He let my nipple drop from his mouth and started attacking my neck. "You know all I need is ten minutes. Once I get up in that sweetness you got down here between your legs,"—his fingers brushed against my swollen nub, and my body trembled—"I can only last but so long."

"I know!" I squealed when he bit my neck and smacked my ass.

"It's good that you know. Now, go lie on the couch over there and open up for me. I'm ready to eat."

I wiggled out of his hold and made my way to the leather couch in the corner of his office. Looking at the time, I knew I had about thirty minutes to spare if I wanted to at least make it to the hospital before traffic started to really pick up. Hopefully, by the time we were done, I'd be able to make it to Diamond no later than forty-five minutes. With Lucci coming from the other side of L.A and Kay Kay coming from Long Beach, I knew we'd probably end up at St. Mary's around the same time. Until then, I was going to enjoy this last fuck and then be on my way.